The Land of Many Colours

Ruskin Bond is known for his signature simplistic and witty writing style. He is the author of several bestselling short stories, novellas, collections, essays and children's books; and has contributed a number of poems and articles to various magazines and anthologies. At the age of 23, he won the prestigious John Llewellyn Rhys Prize for his first novel, *The Room on the Roof.* He was also the recipient of the Padma Shri in 1999, Lifetime Achievement Award by the Delhi Government in 2012 and the Padma Bhushan in 2014.

Born in 1934, Ruskin Bond grew up in Jamnagar, Shimla, New Delhi and Dehradun. Apart from three years in the UK, he has spent all his life in India and now lives in Landour, Mussoorie, with his adopted family.

RUSKIN BOND

The Land of Many Colours

RUPA

Published by
Rupa Publications India Pvt. Ltd 2024
7/16, Ansari Road, Daryaganj
New Delhi 110002

Sales centres:
Bengaluru Chennai
Hyderabad Jaipur Kathmandu
Kolkata Mumbai Prayagraj

This is a work of fiction. Names, characters, places and incidents are either the product of the author's imagination or are used fictitiously and any resemblance to any actual person, living or dead, events or locales is entirely coincidental.

P-ISBN: 978-93-6156-428-4
E-ISBN: 978-93-6156-007-1

First impression 2024

10 9 8 7 6 5 4 3 2 1

Printed in India

CONTENTS

INTRODUCTION

Everyone's definition of India is different. Some associate India with the chilly Himalayas, some with the relentless desert heat, some with the holy waters of the Ganga and some with the deep blue waters of the Indian Ocean. Some cherish the enchanting music of Rajasthan, some the hot chai shared during a road trip in the hills and others remember the glory of the evening prayers in the temples of Varanasi. No matter the differences in landscape, cultures and traditions, most people will agree that all of this—and much more—is *all* India. The beauty of this vibrant nation lies in its variety of festivals and its glorious diversity.

The stories in *The Land of Many Colours* attempt to show this diversity and all the joy it brings. Tales like 'Great Trees of Garhwal' and 'Tales of Old Mussoorie' take you on a trip along the mountains, while those like 'Flowers on the Ganga' and 'Of Rivers and Pilgrims' highlight the beauty and pulsating life along the riverside. Other stories like 'Voting at Barlowganj' and 'Bus Stop, Pipalnagar' give one a chance to see the intricacies of small-town India. There are many other tales as well that celebrate the bright shades of this nation.

The splashes of colourful clothing and the variety of food, especially during the different festivals—such as Bihu, Diwali, Eid, Pongal—make India what it is. Our country contains multitudes, and these stories are only a humble attempt at highlighting as much of it as possible. There is so much written about India, and it is still not enough. The vivid colours and quirks can mean something different for each person, it can teach each one of us different things. I hope the stories here help you reflect on the memories of *your* India in all its diverse glory.

Ruskin Bond

THE INDIA I CARRIED WITH ME

I am now going back in time, to a period when I was caught between East and West, and had to make up my mind just where I belonged. I had been away from India for barely a month before I was longing to return. The insularity of the place where I found myself (Jersey, in the Channel Islands) had something to do with it, I suppose. There was little there to remind me of India or the East, not one brown face to be seen in the streets or on the beaches. I'm sure it's a different sort of place now; but fifty years ago it had nothing to offer by way of companionship or good cheer to a lonely, sensitive boy who had left home and friends in search of a 'better future'.

I had come to England with a dream of sorts, and I was to return to India with another kind of dream; but in between there were to be four years of dreary office work, lonely bed-sitting rooms, shabby lodging houses, cheap snack bars, hospital wards, and the struggle to write my first book and find a publisher for it.

I started work in a large departmental store called *Le Riche.* At eight in the morning, when I walked to the store, it was dark. At six in the evening, when I walked home, it was dark again. Where were all those sunny beaches Jersey was famous for? I would have to wait for summer to see them, and a Saturday afternoon to take a dip in the sea.

Occasionally, after an early supper, I would walk along the deserted seafront. If the tide was in and the wind was approaching gale-force, the waves would climb the sea wall and drench me with their cold salt spray. My aunt, with whom I was staying, thought I was quite mad to take this solitary walk; but I have always been at one with nature, even in its wilder moments, and the wind and the crashing waves gave me a sense of freedom, strengthened my determination to escape from the island and go my own way.

When I wasn't walking along the seafront, I would sit at the portable typewriter in my small attic room, and hammer out the rough chapters of the book that was to become my first novel. These were characters and incidents based on the journal I had kept during my last year in India. It was 1951, recalled in late 1952. An eighteen-year-old looking back on incidents in the life of a seventeen-year-old! Nostalgia and longing suffused those pages. How I longed to be back with my friends in the small town of Dehradun—a leafy place, sunny, fruit-laden, easy-going, every familiar corner etched clearly in my memory. Somehow, it had been that last year in Dehra that had brought me closer to the India that I had so far only taken for granted. An India of close and sometimes sentimental friendships. Of striking contrasts: a small cinema showing English pictures (a George Formby comedy or an American musical) and only a couple of hours away thousands taking a dip in the sacred water of the Ganga. Or outside the station, hundreds of pony-drawn tongas waiting to pick up passengers, while the more affluent climbed into their Ford Convertibles, Morris Minors, Baby Austins or flashy Packards and Daimlers.

But of course Dehra in the 1950s was a town of bicycles. Students, shopkeepers, Army cadets, office workers, all used them. The scooter (or Lambretta) had only just been invented, and it would be several years before it took over from the bicycle. It was still unaffordable for the great majority.

I was awkward on a bicycle and frequently fell off, breaking my arm on one occasion. But this did not prevent me from joining my friends on cycle rides to the sulphur springs, or to Premnagar (where the Military Academy was situated) or along the Haridwar road and down to the riverbed at Lachhiwala.

In Jersey, I found an old cycle belonging to my cousin, and I rode from St Helier, where we lived, to St. Brelade's Bay, at the other end of the island. But returning after dark, I was hauled up for riding without lights. I had no idea that cycles had also to be equipped with lights. Back in Dehra, we never used them!

The attic room had no view, so one of my favourite occupations, gazing out of windows, came to a stop. But perhaps this was helpful in that it made me concentrate on the sheet of paper in my typewriter. After about six months, I had a book of sorts ready for submission to any publisher who was prepared to look at it. Meanwhile, I had been through at least three jobs and had even been offered a post in the Jersey Civil Service, having successfully taken the local civil service exam—something I had done out of sheer boredom, as I had no intention of settling permanently on the island.

I had been keeping a diary of sorts and in some of the entries I had expressed my desire to get back to India, and my discontent at having to stay with relatives who were unsympathetic, not only to my feelings for India but also to my ambitions to become a writer. The diary fell into my uncle's hands. He read it, and was naturally upset. We had a row. I was contrite; but a few days later I packed my suitcases (all two of them) and stepped on to the ferry that was to take me to Southampton and then to London. Lesson one: don't leave your personal diaries lying around!

But perhaps it was all for the best, otherwise I might have hung around in Jersey for another year or two, to the detriment of my personal happiness and my writing ambitions.

I arrived in London in the middle of a thick yellow November fog—those were the days of the killer London fogs—and after a search found the Students' Hostel where I was given a cubicle to myself. But I did not stay there very long; the available food was awful. As soon as I got an office job—not too difficult in the 1950s—I rented an attic room in Belsize Park, the first of many bed-sitters that I was to live in during my three-year sojourn in London.

From Belsize Park I was to move to Haverstock Hill (close to Hampstead Heath), then to South London for a short time, and finally to Swiss Cottage. Most of my landladies were Jewish—refugees from persecution in pre-War Europe—and I too was a refugee of sorts, still very unsure of where I belonged. Was it England, the land of my father, or India, the land of my birth? But my father had also been born in India, had grown up and made a living there, visiting *his* father's land, England, only a couple of times during his life.

The link with Britain was tenuous, based on heredity rather than upbringing. It was more in the mind. It was a literary England I had been drawn to, not a physical England. And in fact, I took several exploratory walks around 'literary' London, visiting houses or streets where famous writers had once lived; in particular the East End and Dockland, for I had grown up on the novels and stories of Dickens, Smollett, Captain Marryat, and W.W. Jacobs. But I did not make many English friends. If they were a reserved race, I was even more reserved. Always shy, I waited for others to take the initiative. In India, people will take the initiative, they lose no time in getting to know you. Not so in England. They were too polite to look at you. And in that respect, I was more English than the English.

The gentleman who lived on the floor below me occasionally

went so far as to greet me with the observation, 'Beastly weather, isn't it?'

And I would respond by saying, 'Oh, perfectly beastly,' and pass on.

How different it was when I bumped into a Gujarati boy, Praveen, who lived on the basement floor. He gave me a winning smile, and I remember saying, 'Oh, to be in Bombay now that winter's here,' and immediately we were friends.

He was only seventeen, a year or two younger than me, and he was studying at one of the polytechnics with a view to getting into the London School of Economics. At that time, most of the Indians in London were students, the great immigration rush was still a long way off, and racial antagonisms were directed more at the recently arrived West Indians than at Asians.

Praveen took me on the rounds of the coffee bars, then proliferating all over London, and introduced me to other students, among them a Vietnamese, called Thanh, who cultivated my friendship because, as he said, 'I want to speak English.' When he discovered that my accent was very un-English (you could have called it Welsh with an Anglo-Indian interaction), he dropped me like a hot brick. He was very frank, he was not interested in friendship, he said, only in improving his accent. I heard later that he'd attached himself to a young journalist from up north, who spoke Broad Yorkshire.

Most evenings I remained in my room and worked on my novel. From being a journal it had become a first person narrative, and now I was turning it into fiction in the third person. The title had also undergone a few changes, but finally I settled on *The Room on the Roof*.

Into it, I put all the love and affection I felt for the friends I had left behind in Dehra. It was more than nostalgia, it was a recreation of the people, places and incidents of that last year in India. I did not want it to fade away. The riverbanks at Haridwar, the mango-groves of the Doon, the poinsettias and bougainvillaea, the games on the parade ground, the chaat shops near the Clock Tower, the summer heat, the monsoon downpours, romping naked in the rain, sitting on railway platforms, gnawing at a stick of sugar cane, listening to street cries... All this and more came crowding upon me as I sat writing before the gas fire in my little room.

When it grew very cold, I used an old overcoat given to me by Diana Athill, the junior partner at Andre Deutsch, who had promised to publish *The Room* if I rewrote it as a novel. Another who encouraged me was a BBC producer, Prudence Smith, who got me to give a couple of talks on Radio's Third Programme. I felt I was getting somewhere; and when I found myself confined to the Hampstead General Hospital for almost a month, with a mysterious disease which had affected the vision in my right eye, I used the left to catch up on my reading and to write a couple of short stories.

A nurse brought a tray of books around the ward every afternoon, and thanks to this courtesy, I was able to discover the delightful stories of William Saroyan and Denton Welch's sensitive first novel *Maiden Voyage.* Saroyan, a Pulitzer Prize winner for his play *The Time of Your Life,* was then very successful and popular. Denton's promising career had been cut short by a terrible accident. Out cycling on a country road, he had been knocked down by a speeding motorist. He had lived for several years, struggling against crippling injuries and almost completing his sensitive autobiography *A Voice in the Clouds.* He was thirty-one when he died. Towards the end, he could only work for three or four minutes at a time. Complications set in, and the left side of his heart started failing. Even then he made a terrific effort to finish his book. His friend Eric wrote—'Denton was upheld by the high courage which seemed somehow the fruit of his rare intelligence.'

The work of these writers, together with the bottle of Guinness I was given every day as a tonic (they had found me somewhat undernourished), meant that I walked out of the hospital with a spring in my step and a determination to succeed.

But Andre Deutsch was still dithering over my book. The firm was doing well, but he didn't like taking risks. No publisher likes losing money. And he wasn't going to make much out of my novel, a subjective and unsensational work.

But I resented his indecision. So I returned the small amount he'd paid me by way of an option, and demanded the return of my manuscript. Back came an apologetic letter and an advance (then £50) against publication.

Today, almost fifty years later, the firm of Andre Deutsch has gone, but *The Room on the Roof* is still in print, still making friends. This is not something that I gloat over, it only goes to show that books are unpredictable commodities, and that the most successful authors and publishers often fall by the wayside. Publishers go out of business, writers fade from the public mind. Even Saroyan is forgotten now. I'll be forgotten too, someday.

There were to be further delays before *The Room* was published, and I was back in India when it did come out. By then I'd almost forgotten about the book! But it picked up the John Llewellyn Rhys Prize, an award that also went to V.S. Naipaul a year later, for his first book. It was then worth only £50. There were no big sponsors in those days. It is now sponsored by a British newspaper and is worth £5,000. This was turned down last year by another Indian writer, who disagreed with the paper's policies.

Meanwhile, in London, there were other distractions. I loved stage musicals, and if I had a little money to spare I went to the theatre, taking in such productions as *Porgy and Bess, Paint Your Wagon, Pal Joey, Teahouse of the August Moon,* and the occasional review. And of course the annual presentation of *Peter Pan* at the Scala Theatre, not far from where I worked. I had grown up on Peter Pan, first read to me by my father in distant Jamnagar, and at school I had read Barrie's other plays and been charmed by them; but, like operetta, they had gone out of fashion and only the ageless Peter remained. 'Do you believe in fairies?' he asks in the play. And to save Tinker Bell from extinction, I clapped with the rest of the audience. But did I really believe in fairies? I looked for them in Kensington Gardens, where Peter Pan's statue stood, and found a few mothers pushing their perambulators, but no fairies. And I looked in Hyde Park, but found only courting couples. And I looked all over Leicester Square, but instead of fairies I found prostitutes soliciting business. As I was still looking for romance, I crept back to my room and my portable typewriter—I would have to create my own romance.

The small portable had been in the windows of a Jersey department store, and every time I passed the store I glanced at the window to see if the typewriter was still there. It seemed to be waiting for me to come in and take it away. I longed to buy it, partly because I had to type out the final drafts of my book, and also because it looked very dainty and attractive. It was definitely out to seduce me. Finally, with the help of a loan from Mr Bromley, a kindly senior clerk, I bought the machine. It cost only £12, but that was three month's wages at the time. It accompanied me to London, and then a couple of years later to India, giving me good service in Dehradun, New Delhi, and then Mussoorie where it finally succumbed to the damp monsoon climate.

My worldly possessions had increased, not only by the

typewriter, but also by a record player which I had bought second-hand from a Thai student. I had become an ardent fan of the Black singer, Eartha Kitt, and had bought all her records; but they were no good without a player until the Thai boy came to my rescue. Then the sensual, throaty voice of Eartha reverberated through the lodging house, bringing complaints from the landlady and the gentleman downstairs. I had to keep the volume low, which wasn't much fun.

I was also fond of the clarinet (turj) playing of an Indian musician, Master Ibrahim, and I had some of his recordings which transported me back to the streets and bazaars of small-town India. Light, lilting and tuneful, I preferred this sort of flute music to the warblings of the more popular songsters.

Praveen liked gangster films and wanted me to accompany him to anything which featured Humphrey Bogart, James Cagney, George Raft and other tough guys. Praveen wanted to be a tough guy himself and often struck a Bogart-like pose, cigarette dangling from the side of his mouth. There was nothing tough about Praveen, who was really rather delicate, but his affectations were charming and risible.

One day he announced that he was returning to India for a few months, as his ailing mother was anxious to see him. He asked me to come along too, to give him company during the three week voyage. To do so, I would have to throw up my job, but I had already thrown up several jobs. They were simply stop-gaps until I could establish myself as a writer. I hadn't the slightest intention or ambition of being a senior clerk or even an executive for the firm in which I was working. The only problem in leaving England then was that I would have to leave my book in limbo, as there was still no guarantee that Deutsch would publish it. But it was time I went on to write other things; time to strike out on my own, to take a chance with

India. The ships were full of British and Anglo-Indian families coming to England, to make a 'better future' for themselves. I would do the opposite, go into reverse, and make my future, for good or ill, in the land of my birth.

My passport was in order, and I had only to give a week's notice to my employers. I had saved up about £200, and of this £50 went on the cost of my passage, London to Bombay. Praveen and I boarded the *S.S. Balory*, a Polish liner with a reputation for running into trouble. We had no difficulty in securing berths in tourist class. Praveen had every intention of returning to England to complete his studies. My own intentions were very vague. I knew there would be no job for me in India, but I was quietly confident that I could make a living from writing, and that too in the English language.

The *Balory* lived up to its reputation. Some of the crew went missing at Gibraltar. A passenger fell overboard in the Red Sea. Lifeboats were lowered, but he could not be found.

Praveen fell in love with an Egyptian girl who disembarked at Aden. He followed her ashore, and I had to run after him and get him back to the ship. As we docked at Ballard Pier, a fire broke out in one of the holds, but by then we were safely ashore. Praveen was swamped by relatives who carried him off to the suburbs of Bombay. I made my way to Victoria Terminus and boarded the Dehradun Express. It was a slow passenger train, which went chugging through several states in the general direction of northern India. Two days and two nights later we crawled through the eastern Doon. It was early March. The mango trees were in blossom, the peacocks were calling, and Belsize Park was far away.

CHILDREN OF INDIA

They pass me every day, on their way to school—boys and girls from the surrounding villages and the outskirts of the hill station. There are no school buses plying for these children: they walk.

For many of them, it's a very long walk to school.

Ranbir, who is ten, has to climb the mountain from his village, four miles distant and 2,000 feet below the town level. He comes in all weathers, wearing the same pair of cheap shoes until they have almost fallen apart.

Ranbir is a cheerful soul. He waves to me whenever he sees me at my window. Sometimes he brings me cucumbers from his father's field. I pay him for the cucumbers; he uses the money for books or for small things needed at home.

Many of the children are like Ranbir—poor, but slightly better off than what their parents were at the same age. They cannot attend the expensive residential and private schools that abound here, but must go to the government-aided schools with only basic facilities. Not many of their parents managed to go to school. They spent their lives working in the fields or delivering milk in the hill station. The lucky ones got into the army. Perhaps Ranbir will do something different when he grows up.

He has yet to see a train but he sees planes flying over the mountains almost every day.

'How far can a plane go?' he asks.

'All over the world,' I tell him. 'Thousands of miles in a day. You can go almost anywhere.'

'I'll go round the world one day,' he vows. 'I'll buy a plane and go everywhere!'

And maybe he will. He has a determined chin and a defiant look in his eye.

The following lines in my journal were put down for my own inspiration or encouragement, but they will do for any determined young person:

> We get out of life what we bring to it. There is not a dream which may not come true if we have the energy which determines our own fate. We can always get what we want if we will it intensely enough…So few people succeed greatly because so few people conceive a great end, working towards it without giving up. We all know that the man who works steadily for money gets rich; the man who works day and night for fame or power reaches his goal. And those who work for deeper, more spiritual achievements will find them too. It may come when we no longer have any use for it, but if we have been willing it long enough, it will come!

◆

Up till a few years ago, very few girls in the hills or in the villages of India went to school. They helped in the home until they were old enough to be married, which wasn't very old. But there are now just as many girls as there are boys going to school.

Bindra is something of an extrovert—a confident fourteen-year-old who chatters away as she hurries down the road with her companions. Her father is a forest guard and knows me quite well: I meet him on my walks through the deodar woods behind Landour. And I had grown used to seeing Bindra almost every day. When she did not put in an appearance for a week, I asked her brother if anything was wrong.

'Oh, nothing,' he says, 'she is helping my mother cut grass. Soon the monsoon will end and the grass will dry up. So we cut it now and store it for the cows for winter.'

'And why aren't you cutting grass, too?'

'Oh, I have a cricket match today,' he says, and hurries away to join his team-mates. Unlike his sister, he puts pleasure before work!

Cricket, once the game of the elite, has become the game of the masses. On any holiday, in any part of this vast country, groups of boys can be seen making their way to the nearest field, or open patch of land, with bat, ball and any other cricketing gear that they can cobble together. Watching some of them play, I am amazed at the quality of talent, at the finesse with which they bat or bowl. Some of the local teams are as good, if not better, than any from the private schools, where there are better facilities. But the boys from these poor or lower-middle-class families will never get the exposure that is necessary to bring them to the attention of those who select state or national teams. They will never get near enough to the men of influence and power. They must continue to play for the love of the game, or watch their more fortunate heroes' exploits on television.

◆

As winter approaches and the days grow shorter, those children who live far away must quicken their pace in order to get home before dark. Ranbir and his friends find that darkness has fallen before they are halfway home.

'What is the time, Uncle?' he asks, as he trudges up the steep road past Ivy Cottage.

One gets used to being called 'Uncle' by almost every boy or girl one meets. I wonder how the custom began. Perhaps it has its origins in the folk tale about the tiger who refrained from pouncing on you if you called him 'uncle'. Tigers don't eat their relatives! Or do they? The ploy may not work if the tiger happens to be a tigress. Would you call her 'Aunty' as she (or your teacher!) descends on you?

It's dark at six and by then, Ranbir likes to be out of the deodar forest and on the open road to the village. The moon and the stars and the village lights are sufficient, but not in the forest, where it is dark even during the day. And the silent flitting of bats and flying foxes, and the eerie hoot of an owl, can be a little disconcerting for the hardiest of children. Once Ranbir and the other boys were chased by a bear.

When he told me about it, I said, 'Well, now we know you can run faster than a bear!'

'Yes, but you have to run downhill when chased by a bear.' He spoke as one having long experience of escaping from bears. 'They run much faster uphill!'

'I'll remember that,' I said, 'thanks for the advice.' And I don't suppose calling a bear 'Uncle' would help.

Usually Ranbir has the company of other boys, and they sing most of the way, for loud singing by small boys will silence owls and frighten away the forest demons. One of them plays a flute, and flute music in the mountains is always enchanting.

◆

Not only in the hills, but all over India, children are constantly making their way to and from school, in conditions that range from dust storms in the Rajasthan desert to blizzards in Ladakh and Kashmir. In the larger towns and cities, there are school buses, but in remote rural areas getting to school can pose a problem.

Most children are more than equal to any obstacles that may arise. Like those youngsters in the Ganjam district of Orissa. In the absence of a bridge, they swim or wade across the Dhanei River every day in order to reach their school. I have a picture of them in my scrapbook. Holding books or satchels aloft in one hand, they do the breast stroke or dog-paddle with the other; or form a chain and help each other across.

Wherever you go in India, you will find children helping out with the family's source of livelihood, whether it be drying fish on the Malabar coast, or gathering saffron buds in Kashmir, or grazing camels or cattle in a village in Rajasthan or Gujarat.

Only the more fortunate can afford to send their children to English-medium private or 'public' schools, and those children really are fortunate, for some of these institutions are excellent schools, as good, and often better, than their counterparts in Britain or the US. Whether it's in Ajmer or Bangalore, New Delhi or Chandigarh, Kanpur or Calcutta, the best schools set very high standards. The growth of a prosperous middle class has led to an ever-increasing demand for quality education. But as private schools proliferate, standards suffer too, and many parents must settle for the second-rate.

The great majority of our children still attend schools run by the state or municipality. These vary from the good to the bad to the ugly, depending on how they are run and where they are situated. A classroom without windows, or with a roof that lets in the monsoon rain, is not uncommon. Even so, children from different communities learn to live and grow together. Hardship makes brothers of us all.

The census tells us that two in every five of the population is in the age group of five to fifteen. Almost half our population is on the way to school!

And here I stand at my window, watching some of them pass

by—boys and girls, big and small, some scruffy, some smart, some mischievous, some serious, but all *going* somewhere—hopefully towards a better future.

THE GREAT INDIAN ROPE TRICK

Everyone has heard of the great Indian rope trick, but I am probably the only person who has actually seen it performed.

It was many years ago, when I was wandering around in the small towns of north India, making a living by writing the occasional story or newspaper article, and staying in cheap hotels or small rented rooms.

I was visiting Kalsi, on the road to Chakrata, with the intention of writing a piece on the rock edicts of the great King Asoka, edicts that had survived in stone for thousands of years.

On a hillock nearby, a small but lively crowd had collected—mostly village folk from the surrounding farmlands—and, like most rustic folk, they were more interested in magic than in history. Come to think of it, so was I!

The object of their interest was a man in a mustard-coloured robe, accompanied by a skinny young boy wearing nothing but a loincloth, or langoti. With the help of his acolyte, the man had been performing various feats of magic, to the amusement of the gathering.

The magician claimed that he could invert the order of nature, and someone in the crowd challenged him to produce out of thin air a bunch of coconuts, well-knowing that coconuts grew by the sea and not in the Himalayan foothills.

'Well, you won't find coconuts growing here,' said the

magician, 'but perhaps there are some to be found above the clouds, in the land of the Gods.'

'But how are we to fetch them?' asked the boy.

'I have the means,' said the man, and proceeded to take from a large round tin box, a cord some tens of feet in length. After carefully arranging the cord, he threw one end of it high up in the air—and there, to everyone's astonishment, it remained as if caught by something. He now paid out the corded rope, which kept going up higher and higher until it disappeared in the mist, leaving only a short length in his hands. He then told the crowd that as he was too heavy to climb the rope himself, he would ask the boy to do so. And handing the end of the rope to the boy, he told him to go ahead.

At first the boy demurred, saying that if he fell from a great height, he would surely be killed. But on being thumped on the head by his angry mentor, he seized the rope and swarmed up it, looking rather like a small spider running up a hanging thread from a wall.

In a few moments, the boy was out of sight, and the crowd fell silent, wondering what would happen next.

Presently, down fell a large coconut—a real coconut—which the pleased magician presented to someone in the crowd. It was followed by several more coconuts.

Then, suddenly, the rope came down, without the boy, and the magician shrieked, 'Someone has cut the rope! What will my boy do now?'

A minute later, down came the boy's head. It bounced on the ground, like a coconut.

This was followed by the boy's arms, legs and body, all falling to the ground one after another.

The mesmerized crowd had been watching these startling events in horror and amazement when suddenly the lid of the tin box flew open and the boy popped out and bowed to the crowd.

A cheer went up, and coins were thrown to the smiling performers. They thanked the crowd with folded hands.

How had they done this trick—if indeed it was a trick? Mesmerism, hypnotism, the powers of suggestion?

The coil of rope was back in its box; the fallen limbs were nowhere to be seen.

As the magician passed me, he smiled and held out a coconut, which I took in both hands. It seemed to quiver as I held it!

Then, as I looked down at the coconut, I saw it change into a human face. Two eyes looked out at me, and a wide mouth broke into a sly grin. This transformation lasted only for seconds, and then it was a coconut again.

I dropped the coconut. It rolled away, and was seized upon by several street urchins, who made off with it.

I turned to see if the magician was still around, and was just in time to catch a glimpse of the man and the boy and the tin box as they disappeared into the crowd—into the mystery and multitude that was India.

OF RIVERS AND PILGRIMS

It's a funny thing, but long before I arrive at a place I can usually tell whether I am going to like it or not. Thus, while I was still some twenty miles from the district town of Pauri, I felt it was not going to be my sort of place, and sure enough it wasn't. A seedy, overgrown place, with too many government offices. On the other hand, while Nandprayag was still out of sight, I knew I was going to like it. And I did.

Perhaps, it's something in the wind—emanations of an atmosphere—that carry to me well before I arrive at my destination. I can't really explain it, and of course it's silly to make judgements in advance. But it does happen.

Anyway, I felt I was nearing home as soon as the bus brought me into the cheerful roadside hamlet, a little way above the Nandakini River's confluence with the Alaknanda. A prayag is a meeting place of two rivers, hence Nandprayag, the place where these two mountain rivers meet. As there are many rivers in the Garhwal Himalayas, all linking up to join either the Ganga or the Yamuna, it follows that there are numerous prayags, in themselves places of pilgrimage as well as wayside halts en route to the higher Hindu shrines at Kedarnath and Badrinath. Nowhere else in these mountains are there so many temples, sacred streams, holy places, and holy men.

Some little way above Nandprayag's sleepy little bazaar is a tourist rest house. It has a well-kept garden surrounded by fruit trees and is a little distance from the general hubbub of the main road.

Above it is the old pilgrim path. Just over twenty years ago, if you were a pilgrim intent on seeking salvation at the abode of the gods, you travelled on foot all the way from the plains, climbing about 200 miles in a couple of months. Those pilgrims had the time, the faith, and the endurance. Illness and misadventure often dogged their footsteps, but what was a little suffering if at the end of the day they arrived at the very portals of heaven?

Today's pilgrims may not be lacking in devotion, but most of them do expect to come home again.

Along the old pilgrim path are several handsome houses, set among mango trees and the fronds of the papaya and banana. Higher up the hill the pine forests commence, but down here it is almost subtropical. Nandprayag is only about 3,000 feet above sea level—a height at which the vegetation is usually lush provided there is protection from the wind.

In one of these double-storeyed houses lives Devki Nandan, a scholar and recluse. He welcomes me into his home and plies me with food till I am close to bursting. He has a great love for this little corner of Garhwal and proudly shows me his collection of cuttings of articles about the area. One is from a travelogue by Sister Nivedita—an Englishwoman, Margaret Noble, who became an interpreter of Hinduism to the West. Visiting Nandprayag in 1928, she wrote:

> Nandprayag is a place that ought to be famous for its beauty and order. For a mile or two before reaching it we had noticed the superior character of the agriculture and even some careful gardening of fruits and vegetables. The peasantry also suddenly grew handsome, not unlike

> the Kashmiris. The town itself is new, rebuilt since the Gohna flood, and its temple stands far out across the fields on the shore of the Prayag. But in this short time a wonderful energy has been at work on architectural carvings and the little place is full of gem-like beauties. As the road crosses the river, I noticed two or three old Pathan tombs, the only traces of Mohammedanism that we had seen north of Srinagar in Garhwal.

Little has changed since Sister Nivedita's visit. There is still a small and thriving Pathan population in Nandprayag. In fact, when I called on Mr Nandan, he was in the act of sending out Eid greetings to his Muslim friends. Some of the old graves have disappeared in the debris from new road cuttings. As for the beautiful temple described by Sister Nivedita, I learned that it had been swept away by a mighty flood in 1970 when a cloudburst and subsequent landslide up-river resulted in great destruction downstream.

◆

Mr Nandan remembers the time when he walked to the small hill station of Pauri to join the old Messmore Christian Mission School, where so many famous sons of Garhwal received their early education. It took him four days marching to get to Pauri. Now it is just four hours by bus. It was only after the Chinese invasion of 1962 that there was a sudden spurt in road building in the northern hill districts. Before that, everyone walked and thought nothing of it.

Sitting on my own that same evening in the little garden of the rest house, I heard innumerable birds break into song. I did not see them, because the light was fading and the trees were dark; but I heard the rather melancholy call of the hill dove, the ascending trill of the koel, and much shrieking, whistling, and twittering that I could not assign to any particular species.

Now, once again, while I sit on the lawn surrounded by zinnias in full bloom, I am teased by that feeling of having been here before, on this lush hillside, among the pomegranates and oleanders. Is it some childhood memory asserting itself? As far as I know, I never travelled in these parts.

It's true that Nandprayag resembles some parts of the Doon Valley (where I grew up) before the Doon was submerged by a tidal wave of humanity. But in the Doon there is no great river running past your garden. Here there are two, and they are also part of this feeling of belonging.

◆

Presently, the room boy joins me for a chat on the lawn. He is in fact running the rest house in the absence of the manager. Wherever I go in India, the manager is usually absent; it seems to make no difference. A coach load of pilgrims is due at any moment, but until they arrive the place is empty and only the birds can be heard.

The room boy's name is Janakpal and he tells me something about his village on the next mountain, where a marauding leopard has been carrying off goats and cattle. He doesn't think much of the laws protecting leopards—nothing can be done unless the animal becomes a man-eater.

A shower of rain descends on us, and so do the pilgrims. Janakpal leaves me to attend to his duties. But I am not left alone for long. A youngster with a cup of tea is the next to interview me. He wants me to take him to Mussoorie or New Delhi. He is fed up, he says, with washing dishes here.

'You are better off here,' I tell him sincerely. 'In Mussoorie you will have twice as many dishes to wash. In Delhi, ten times as many.'

'Yes, but there are cinemas and video and TV there,' he says, leaving me without an argument. Bird song may have charms for me, but not for the restless dishwasher in tranquil Nandprayag.

The rain stops and I go for a walk. The pilgrims keep to themselves, but the locals are always ready to talk. I remember a saying (and it may have originated in these hills), which goes: 'All men are my friends. I have only to meet them.' In Nandprayag, where life still moves at a leisurely and civilized pace, one is constantly meeting them.

BUS STOP, PIPALNAGAR

I

My balcony was my window to the world.

The room itself had only one window, a square hole in the wall crossed by two iron bars. The view from it was rather restricted. If I craned my neck sideways, and put my nose to the bars, I could see the end of the building. Below was a narrow courtyard where children played. Across the courtyard, level with my room, were three separate windows belonging to three separate rooms, each window barred in the same way, with iron bars. During the day it was difficult to see into these rooms. The harsh, cruel sunlight filled the courtyard, making the windows patches of darkness.

My room was very small. I had paced about in it so often that I knew its exact measurements. My foot, from heel to toe, was eleven inches long. That made my room just over fifteen feet in length; for, when I measured the last foot, my toes turned up against the wall. It wasn't more than eight feet broad, which meant that two people was the most it could comfortably accommodate. I was the only tenant but at times I had put up at least three friends—two on the floor, two on the bed. The plaster had been peeling off the walls and in addition the greasy stains and patches were difficult to hide, though I covered the worst ones with pictures cut out from magazines—Waheeda Rehman, the Indian actress, successfully blotted out one big patch and a recent Mr Universe displayed his muscles from the opposite wall. The biggest stain was all but concealed by a calendar that showed Ganesh, the elephant-headed god, whose blessings were vital to all good beginnings.

My belongings were few. A shelf on the wall supported an untidy pile of paperbacks, and a small table in one corner of the room supported the solid weight of my rejected manuscripts and an ancient typewriter which I had obtained on hire.

I was eighteen years old and a writer.

Such a combination would be disastrous enough anywhere, but in India it was doubly so; for there were not many papers to write for and payments were small. In addition, I was very inexperienced and though what I wrote came from the heart, only a fraction touched the hearts of editors. Nevertheless, I persevered and was able to earn about a hundred rupees a month, barely enough to keep body, soul and typewriter together. There wasn't much else I could do. Without that passport to a job—a university degree—I had no alternative but to accept the classification of 'self-employed'—which was impressive as it included doctors, lawyers, property dealers, and grain merchants, most of whom earned well over a thousand rupees a month.

'Haven't you realized that India is bursting with young people trying to pass exams?' asked a journalist friend. 'It's a desperate matter, this race for academic qualifications. Everyone wants to pass his exam the easy way, without reading too many books or attending more than half-a-dozen lectures. That's where a smart fellow like you comes in! Why would students wade through five volumes of political history when they can buy a few model answer papers at any bookstall? They are helpful, these guess papers. You can write them quickly and flood the market. They'll sell like hot cakes!'

'Who eats hot cakes here?'

'Well, then, hot chapattis.'

'I'll think about it,' I said; but the idea repelled me. If I was going to misguide students, I would rather do it by writing second-rate detective stories than by providing them with readymade answer papers. Besides, I thought it would bore me.

II

The string of the cot needed tightening. The dip in the middle of the bed was so bad that I woke up in the morning with a stiff back. But I was hopeless at tightening bed-strings and would have to wait until one of the boys from the tea shop paid me a visit. I was too tall for the cot, anyway, and if my feet didn't stick out at one end, my head lolled over the other.

Under the cot was my tin trunk. Apart from my clothes, it contained notebooks, diaries, photographs, scrapbooks, and other odds and ends that form a part of a writer's existence.

I did not live entirely alone. During cold or rainy weather, the boys from the tea shop, who normally slept on the pavement, crowded into the room. Apart from them, there were lizards on the walls and ceilings—friends these—and a large rat—definitely an enemy—who got in and out of the window and who sometimes carried away manuscripts and clothing.

June nights were the most uncomfortable. Mosquitoes emerged from all the ditches, gullies and ponds, to swarm over Pipalnagar. Bugs, finding it uncomfortable inside the woodwork of the cot, scrambled out at night and found their way under the sheet. The lizards wandered listlessly over the walls, impatient for the monsoon rains, when they would be able to feast off thousands of insects.

Everyone in Pipalnagar was waiting for the cool, quenching relief of the monsoon.

III

I woke every morning at five as soon as the first bus moved out of the shed, situated only twenty or thirty yards down the road. I dressed, went down to the tea shop for a glass of hot tea and some buttered toast, and then visited Deep Chand the barber in his shop.

At eighteen, I shaved about three times a week. Sometimes I shaved myself. But often, when I felt lazy, Deep Chand shaved me, at the special concessional rate of two annas.

'Give my head a good massage, Deep Chand,' I said. 'My brain is not functioning these days. In my latest story there are three murders, but it is boring just the same.'

'You must write a good book,' said Deep Chand, beginning the ritual of the head massage, his fingers squeezing my temples and tugging at my hair-roots. 'Then you can make some money and clear out of Pipalnagar. Delhi is the place to go! Why, I know a man who arrived in Delhi in 1947 with nothing but the clothes he wore and a few rupees. He began by selling thirsty travellers glasses of cold water at the railway station, then he opened a small tea shop; now he has two big restaurants and lives in a house as large as the prime minister's!'

Nobody intended to live in Pipalnagar forever. Delhi was the city most aspired to but as it was 200 miles away, few could afford to travel there.

Deep Chand would have shifted his trade to another town if he had had the capital. In Pipalnagar his main customers were small shopkeepers, factory workers and labourers from the railway station. 'Here I can charge only six annas for a haircut,' he lamented. 'In Delhi I could charge a rupee.'

IV

I was walking in the wheat fields beyond the railway tracks when I noticed a boy lying across the footpath, his head and shoulders hidden by wheat plants. I walked faster, and when I came near I saw that the boy's legs were twitching. He seemed to be having some kind of fit. The boy's face was white, his legs kept moving and his hands fluttered restlessly among the wheat stalks.

'What's the matter?' I said, kneeling down beside him but he was still unconscious.

I ran down the path to a Persian well, and dipping the end of my shirt in a shallow trough of water, soaked it well before returning to the boy. As I sponged his face the twitching ceased, and though he still breathed heavily, his face was calm and his hands still. He opened his eyes and stared at me, but he didn't really see me.

'You have bitten your tongue,' I said, wiping a little blood from the corner of his mouth. 'Don't worry. I'll stay here with you until you are all right.'

The boy raised himself and, resting his chin on his knees, he passed his arms around his drawn-up legs.

'I'm all right now,' he said.

'What happened?' I asked, sitting down beside him.

'Oh, it is nothing, it often happens. I don't know why. I cannot control it.'

'Have you been to a doctor?'

'Yes, when the fits first started, I went to the hospital. They gave me some pills that I had to take every day. But the pills made me so tired and sleepy that I couldn't work properly. So I stopped taking them. Now this happens once or twice a week. What does it matter? I'm all right when it's over and I do not feel anything when it happens.'

He got to his feet, dusting his clothes and smiling at me. He was a slim boy, long-limbed and bony. There was a little fluff on his cheeks and the promise of a moustache. He told me his name was Suraj, that he went to a night school in the city, and that he hoped to finish his high school exams in a few months' time. He was studying hard, he said, and if he passed he hoped to get a scholarship to a good college. If he failed, there was only the prospect of continuing in Pipalnagar.

I noticed a small tray of merchandise lying on the ground. It contained combs and buttons and little bottles of perfume. The tray was made to hang at Suraj's waist, supported by straps that went around his shoulders. All day he walked about Pipalnagar, sometimes covering ten or fifteen miles, selling odds and ends to people in their houses. He averaged about two rupees a day, which was enough for his food and other necessities; he managed to save about ten rupees a month for his school fees. He ate irregularly at little tea shops, at the stall near the bus stop, under the shady jamun and mango trees. When the jamun fruit was ripe, he would sit on a tree, sucking the sour fruit until his lips were stained purple. There was a small, nagging fear that he might get a fit while sitting on the tree and fall off, but the temptation to eat jamun was greater than his fear.

All this he told me while we walked through the fields towards the bazaar.

'Where do you live?' I asked. 'I'll walk home with you.'

'I don't live anywhere,' said Suraj. 'My home is not in Pipalnagar. Sometimes I sleep at the temple or at the railway station. In the summer months I sleep on the grass of the municipal park.'

'Well, wherever it is you stay, let me come with you.'

We walked together into the town, and parted near the

bus stop. I returned to my room, and tried to do some writing while Suraj went to the bazaar to try selling his wares. We had agreed to meet each other again. I realized that Suraj was an epileptic, but there was nothing unusual about him being an orphan and a refugee. I liked his positive attitude to life. Most people in Pipalnagar were resigned to their circumstances but he was ambitious. I also liked his gentleness, his quiet voice, and the smile that flickered across his face regardless of whether he was sad or happy.

V

The temperature had touched forty-three degrees Celsius, and the small streets of Pipalnagar were empty. To walk barefoot on the scorching pavements was possible only for labourers, whose feet had developed several hard layers of protective skin; and now even these hardy men lay stretched out in the shade provided by trees and buildings.

I hadn't written anything in two weeks, and though one or two small payments were due from a Delhi newspaper, I could think of no substantial amount that was likely to come my way in the near future. I decided that I would dash off a couple of articles that same night, and post them the following morning.

Having made this comforting decision, I lay down on the floor in preference to the cot. I liked the touch of things; the touch of a cool floor on a hot day, the touch of earth—soft, grassy grass was good, especially dew-drenched grass. Wet earth was soft, sensuous, as was splashing through puddles and streams.

I slept, and dreamt of a cool, clear stream in a forest glade, where I bathed in gay abandon. A little further downstream was another bather. I hailed him, expecting to see Suraj but when the bather turned I found that it was my landlord's pot-bellied rent collector, holding an accounts ledger in his hands.

This woke me up, and for the remainder of the day I worked feverishly at my articles.

Next morning, when I opened the door, I found Suraj asleep at the top of the steps. His tray lay at the bottom of the steps. He woke up as soon as I touched his shoulder.

'Have you been sleeping here all night?' I asked. 'Why didn't you come in?'

'It was very late,' said Suraj. 'I didn't want to disturb you.'

'Someone could have stolen your things while you were asleep.'

'Oh, I sleep quite lightly. Besides I have nothing of great value. But I came here to ask you a favour.'

'You need money?'

He laughed. 'Do all your friends mean money when they ask for favours? No, I want you to take your meal with me tonight.'

'But where? You have no place of your own and it would be too expensive in a restaurant.'

'In your room,' said Suraj. 'I shall bring the meat and vegetables and cook them here. Do you have a cooker?'

'I think so,' I said, scratching my head in some perplexity. 'I will have to look for it.'

Suraj brought a chicken for dinner—a luxury, one to be indulged in only two or three times a year. He had bought the bird for seven rupees, which was cheap. We spiced it and roasted it on a spit.

'I wish we could do this more often,' I said, as I dug my teeth into the soft flesh of a second chicken leg.

'We could do it at least once a month if we worked hard,' said Suraj.

'You know how to work. You work from morning to evening and then you work again.'

'But you are a writer. That is different. You have to wait for the right moment.'

I laughed. 'Moods and moments are for geniuses. No, it's really a matter of working hard, and I'm just plain lazy, to tell you the truth.'

'Perhaps you are writing the wrong things.'

'Perhaps, I wish I could do something else. Even if I repaired bicycle tyres, I'd make more money!'

'Then why don't you repair bicycle tyres?'

'Oh, I would rather be a bad writer than a good repairer of cycle tyres.' I brightened up, 'I could go into business, though. Do you know I once owned a vegetable stall?'

'Wonderful! When was that?'

'A couple of months ago. But it failed after two days.'

'Then you are not good at business. Let us think of something else.'

'I can tell fortunes with cards.'

'There are already too many fortune tellers in Pipalnagar.'

'Then we won't talk of fortunes. And you must sleep here tonight. It is better than sleeping on the roadside.'

VI

At noon when the shadows shifted and crossed the road, a band of children rushed down the empty street, shouting and waving their satchels. They had been at their desks from early morning, and now, despite the hot sun, they would have their fling while their elders slept on string charpoys beneath leafy neem trees.

On the soft sand near the riverbed, boys wrestled or played leapfrog. At alley corners, where tall buildings shaded narrow passages, the favourite game was gulli-danda. The gulli—a small piece of wood, about four inches long sharpened to a point at each end—is struck with the danda—a short, stout stick. A player is allowed three hits, and his score is the distance, in danda lengths, of his hits of the gulli. Boys who were experts at the game sent the gulli flying far down the road—sometimes into a shop or through a windowpane, which resulted in confusion, loud invective, and a dash for cover.

A game for both children and young men was kabaddi. This is a game that calls for good breath control and much agility. It is also known in different parts of India as hootoo-too, kho-kho and atya patya. Ramu, Deep Chand's younger brother, excelled at this game. He was the Pipalnagar kabaddi champion.

The game is played by two teams, consisting of eight or nine members each, who face each other across a dividing line. Each side in turn sends out one of its players into the opponent's area. This person has to keep on saying 'kabaddi, kabaddi' very fast and without taking a second breath. If he returns to his side after touching an opponent, that opponent is 'dead' and out of the game. If, however, he is caught and cannot struggle back to his side while still holding his breath, he is 'dead'.

Ramu, who was also a good wrestler, knew all the kabaddi holds, and was particularly good at capturing opponents. He had vitality and confidence, rare things in Pipalnagar. He wanted to go into the army after finishing school, a happy choice I thought.

VII

Suraj did not know if his parents were dead or alive. He had literally lost them when he was six. His father had been a farmer, a dark, unfathomable man who spoke little, thought perhaps even less and was vaguely aware he had a son—a weak boy given to introspection and dawdling at the riverbank when he should have been helping in the fields.

Suraj's mother had been a subdued, silent woman, frail and consumptive. Her husband seemed to expect that she would not live long, but Suraj did not know if she was living or dead. He had lost his parents at Amritsar railway station in the days of Partition, when trains coming across the border from Pakistan disgorged themselves of thousands of refugees or pulled into the station half-empty, drenched with blood and littered with corpses.

Suraj and his parents had been lucky to escape one of these massacres. Had they travelled on an earlier train (which they had tried desperately to catch), they might have been killed. Suraj was clinging to his mother's sari while she tried to keep up with her husband who was elbowing his way through the frightened, bewildered throng of refugees. Suraj collided with a burly Sikh and lost his grip on the sari. The Sikh had a long curved sword at his waist, and Suraj stared up at him in awe and fascination—at the man's long hair, which had fallen loose, at his wild black beard, and at the bloodstains on his white shirt. The Sikh pushed him aside and when Suraj looked around for his mother, she was not to be seen. She was hidden from him by a mass of restless bodies, all pushing in different directions. He could hear her calling his name and he tried to force his way through the crowd in the direction of her voice, but he was carried on the other way.

At night, when the platform emptied, he was still searching for his mother. Eventually, the police came and took him away. They looked for his parents but without success, and finally they sent him to a home for orphans. Many children lost their parents at about the same time.

Suraj stayed at the orphanage for two years and when he was eight, and felt himself a man, he ran away. He worked for some time as a helper in a tea shop; but when he started having epileptic fits the shopkeeper asked him to leave, and the boy found himself on the streets, begging for a living. He begged for a year, moving from one town to the next and finally ended up in Pipalnagar. By then he was twelve and really too old to beg, but he had saved some money, and with it he bought a small stock of combs, buttons, cheap perfumes and bangles, and, converting himself into a mobile shop, went from door to door selling his wares.

Pipalnagar is a small town and there was no house which Suraj hadn't visited. Everyone knew him; some had offered him food and drink; and the children liked him because he often played on a small flute when he went on his rounds.

VIII

Suraj came to see me quite often and, when he stayed late, he slept in my room, curling up on the floor and sleeping fitfully. He would always leave early in the morning before I could get him anything to eat.

'Should I go to Delhi, Suraj?' I asked him one evening.

'Why not? In Delhi, there are many ways of making money.'

'And spending it too. Why don't you come with me?'

'After my exams, perhaps. Not now.'

'Well, I can wait. I don't want to live alone in a big city.'

'In the meantime, write your book.'

'All right, I will try.'

We decided we could try to save a little money from Suraj's earnings and my own occasional payments from newspapers and magazines. Even if we were to give Delhi only a few days' trial, we would need money to live on. We managed to put away twenty rupees one week, but withdrew it the next when a friend, Pitamber, asked for a loan to repair his cycle rickshaw. He returned the money in three instalments but we could not save any of it. Pitamber and Deep Chand also had plans of going to Delhi. Pitamber wanted to own his own cycle rickshaw; Deep Chand dreamt of a swanky barber shop in the capital.

One day Suraj and I hired bicycles and rode out of Pipalnagar. It was a hot, sunny morning and we were perspiring after we had gone two miles, but a fresh wind sprang up suddenly, and we could smell the rain in the air though there were no clouds to be seen.

'Let us go where there are no people at all,' said Suraj. 'I am a little tired of people. I see too many of them all day.'

We got down from our cycles and, pushing them off the road, took a path through a paddy field and then one through a field of young maize, and in the distance we saw a tree, a crooked tree, growing beside a well. I do not even today know the name of that tree. I had never seen its kind before. It had a crooked trunk, crooked branches and it was clothed in thick, broad, crooked leaves, like the leaves on which food is served in bazaars.

In the trunk of the tree was a large hole and when I sat my cycle down with a crash, two green parrots flew out of the hole, and went dipping and swerving across the fields.

There was grass around the well, cropped short by grazing cattle, so we sat in the shade of the crooked tree and Suraj untied the red cloth in which we had brought food. We ate our bread and vegetable curry; meanwhile the parrots returned to the tree.

'Let us come here every week,' said Suraj, stretching himself out on the grass. It was a drowsy day, the air was humid and he soon fell asleep. I was aware of different sensations. I heard a cricket singing in the tree; the cooing of pigeons which lived in the walls of the old well; the soft breathing of Suraj; a rustling in the leaves of the tree; the distant drone of the bees. I smelt the grass and the old bricks around the well, and the promise of rain.

When I opened my eyes, I saw dark clouds on the horizon. Suraj was still sleeping with his arms thrown across his face to keep the glare out of his eyes. As I was thirsty, I went to the well and, putting my shoulders to it, turned the wheel very slowly, walking around the well four times, while cool clean water gushed out over the stones and along the channel to the fields. I drank from one of the trays, and the water tasted sweet; the deeper the wells, the sweeter the water. Suraj was sitting up now, looking at the sky.

'It's going to rain,' he said.

We pushed our cycles back to the main road and began riding homewards. We were a mile out of Pipalnagar when it began to rain. A lashing wind swept the rain across our faces, but we exulted in it and sang at the top of our voices until we reached the bus stop. Leaving the cycles at the hire shop, we ran up the rickety, swaying steps to my room.

In the evening, as the bazaar was lighting up, the rain stopped. We went to sleep quite early, but at midnight I was woken by the moon shining full on my face—a full moon, shedding its light all over Pipalnagar, peeping and prying into every home, washing the empty streets, silvering the corrugated tin roofs.

IX

The lizards hung listlessly on the walls and ceilings, waiting for the monsoon rains, which bring out all the insects from their cracks and crannies.

One day, clouds loomed upon the horizon, growing rapidly into enormous towers. A faint breeze sprang up, bringing with it the first of the monsoon raindrops. This was the moment everyone was waiting for. People ran out of their houses to take in the fresh breeze and the scent of those first few raindrops on the parched, dusty earth. Underground, in their cracks, the insects were moving. Termites and white ants, which had been sleeping through the hot season, emerged from their lairs.

And then, on the second or third night of the monsoon, came the great yearly flight of insects into the cool, brief freedom of the night. Out of every crack, from under the roots of trees, huge winged ants emerged, at first fluttering about heavily, on the first and last flight of their lives. At night there was only one direction in which they could fly—towards the light; towards the electric bulbs and smoky kerosene lamps throughout Pipalnagar. The street lamp opposite the bus stop, beneath my room, attracted a massive, quivering swarm of clumsy termites, which gave the impression of one thick, slowly-revolving body.

This was the hour of the lizards. Now they had their reward for those days of patient waiting. Plying their sticky pink tongues, they devoured the insects as fast as they came. For hours, they crammed their stomachs, knowing that such a feast would not be theirs again for another year. How wasteful nature is, I thought. Through the whole hot season the insect world prepares for the flight out of the darkness into light and not one of them survives its freedom.

Suraj and I walked barefooted over the cool, wet pavements, across the railway lines and the riverbed, until we were not far from the crooked tree. Dotting the landscape were old abandoned brick kilns. When it rained heavily, the hollows made by the kilns filled up with water. Suraj and I found a small tank where we could bathe and swim. On a mound in the middle of the tank stood a ruined hut, formerly inhabited by a watchman at the kiln. We swam and then wrestled on the young green grass. Though I was heavier than Suraj and my chest as sound as a new drum, he had a lot of power in his long, wiry arms and legs, and he pinioned me about the waist with his bony knees. And then suddenly, as I strained to press his back to the ground, I felt his body go tense. He stiffened, his thigh jerked against me and his legs began to twitch. I knew that a fit was coming on, but I was unable to get out of his grip. He held me more tightly as the fit took possession of him.

When I noticed his mouth working, I thrust the palm of my hand in, sideways, to prevent him from biting his tongue. But so violent was the convulsion that his teeth bit into my flesh. I shouted with pain and tried to pull my hand away, but he was unconscious and his jaw was set. I closed my eyes and counted slowly up to seven and then I felt his muscles relax and I was able to take my hand away. It was bleeding a little but I bound it with a handkerchief before Suraj fully regained consciousness.

He didn't say much as we walked back to town. He looked depressed and weak, but I knew it wouldn't take long for him to recover his usual good spirits. He did not notice that I kept my hand out of sight and only after he had returned from classes that night did he notice the bandage and asked what happened.

X

'Do you want to make some money?' asked Pitamber, bursting into the room like a festive cracker.

'I do,' I said.

'What do we have to do for it?' asked Suraj, striking a cautious note.

'Oh nothing, carry a banner and walk in front of a procession.'

'Why?'

'Don't ask me. Some political stunt.'

'Which party?'

'I don't know. Who cares? All I know is that they are paying two rupees a day to anyone who'll carry a flag or banner.'

'We don't need two rupees that badly,' I said. 'And you can make more than that in a day with your rickshaw.'

'True, but they're paying me *five.* They're fixing a loudspeaker to my rickshaw, and one of the party's men will sit in it and make speeches as we go along. Come on, it will be fun.'

'No banners for us,' I said. 'But we may come along and watch.'

And we did watch, when, later that morning, the procession passed along our street. It was a ragged procession of about a hundred people, shouting slogans. Some of them were children, and some of them were men who did not know what it was all about, but all joined in the slogan-shouting.

We didn't know much about it, either. Because, though the man in Pitamber's rickshaw was loud and eloquent, his loudspeaker was defective, with the result that his words were punctuated with squeaks and an eerie whining sound. Pitamber looked up and saw us standing on the balcony and gave us a wave and a wide grin. We decided to follow the procession at a discreet distance. It was a protest march against something or other; we never did manage to find out the details. The destination was the municipal office, and by the time we got there the crowd had increased to two or three hundred people. Some rowdies had now joined in, and things began to get out of hand. The man in the rickshaw continued his speech; another man standing on a wall was making a speech; and someone from the municipal office was confronting the crowd and making a speech of his own.

A stone was thrown, then another. From a sprinkling of stones, it soon became a shower of stones; and then some police constables, who had been standing by watching the fun, were ordered into action. They ran at the crowd where it was thinnest, brandishing stout sticks.

We were caught in the stampede that followed. A stone—flung no doubt at a policeman—was badly aimed and struck me on the shoulder. Suraj pulled me down a side street. Looking back, we saw Pitamber's cycle rickshaw lying on its side in the middle of the road, but there was no sign of Pitamber.

Later, he turned up in my room, with a cut over his left eyebrow which was bleeding freely. Suraj washed the cut, and I poured iodine over it—Pitamber did not flinch—and covered it with sticking plaster. The cut was quite deep and should have had stitches, but Pitamber was superstitious about hospitals, saying he knew very few people to come out of them alive. He was of course thinking about the Pipalnagar hospital.

So he acquired a scar on his forehead. It went rather well with his demonic good looks.

XI

'Thank God for the monsoon,' said Suraj. 'We won't have any more demonstrations on the roads until the weather improves!'

And, until the rain stopped, Pipalnagar was fresh and clean and alive. The children ran naked out of their houses and romped through the streets. The gutters overflowed, and the road became a mountain stream, coursing merrily towards the bus stop.

At the bus stop there was confusion. Newly arrived passengers, surrounded on all sides by a sea of mud and rainwater, were met by scores of tongas and cycle rickshaws, each jostling the other trying to cater to the passengers. As a result, only half found conveyances, while the other half found themselves knee-deep in Pipalnagar mud.

Pipalnagar mud has a quality all its own—and it is not easily removed or forgotten. Only buffaloes love it because it is soft and squelchy. Two parts of it are thick, sticky clay which seems to come alive at the slightest touch, clinging tenaciously to human flesh. Feet sink into it and have to be wrenched out. Fingers become webbed. Get it into your hair, and there is nothing you can do except go to Deep Chand and have your head shaved.

London has its fog, Paris its sewers, Pipalnagar its mud. Pitamber, of course, succeeded in getting as his passenger the most attractive girl to step off the bus, and showed her his skill and daring by taking her to her destination by the longest and roughest road.

The rain swirled over the trees and roofs of the town, and the parched earth soaked it up, giving out a fresh smell that came only once a year, the fragrance of quenched earth, that loveliest of all smells.

In my room I was battling against the elements, for the door would not close, and the rain swept into the room and soaked my cot. When finally I succeeded in closing the door, I discovered that the roof was leaking and the water was trickling down the walls, running through the dusty design I had made with my feet. I placed tins and mugs in strategic positions and, satisfied that everything was now under control, sat on the cot to watch the rooftops through my windows.

There was a loud banging on the door. It flew open, and there was Suraj standing on the threshold, drenched. Coming in, he began to dry himself while I made desperate efforts to close the door again.

'Let's make some tea,' he said.

Glasses of hot, sweet milky tea on a rainy day...it was enough to make me feel fresh and full of optimism. We sat on the cot, enjoying the brew.

'One day, I'll write a book,' I said. 'Not just a thriller, but a real book, about real people. Perhaps about you and me and Pipalnagar. And then we'll be famous and our troubles will be over and new troubles will begin. I don't mind problems as long as they are new. While you're studying, I'll write my book. I'll start tonight. It is an auspicious time, the first night of the monsoon.'

A tree must have fallen across the wires somewhere, because the lights would not come on. So I lit a small oil lamp, and while it spluttered in the steamy darkness Suraj opened his book and, with one hand on the book, the other playing with his toe—this helped him to concentrate!—he began to study. I took the inkpot down from the shelf, and finding it empty, added a little rainwater to it from one of the mugs. I sat down beside Suraj and began to write, but the pen was no good and made blotches all over the paper. And, although I was full of writing just then, I didn't really know what I wanted to say.

So I went out and began pacing up and down the road. There I found Pitamber, a little drunk, very merry, and prancing about in the middle of the road.

'What are you dancing for?' I asked.

'I'm happy, so I'm dancing,' said Pitamber.

'And why are you happy?' I asked.

'Because I'm dancing,' he said.

The rain stopped and the neem trees gave out a strong, sweet smell.

XII

Flowers in Pipalnagar—did they exist? As a child I knew a garden in Lucknow where there were beds of phlox and petunias and another garden where only roses grew. In the fields around Pipalnagar was thorn apple—a yellow buttercup nestling among thorn leaves. But in Pipalnagar Bazaar there were no flowers except one—a marigold growing out of a crack on my balcony. I had removed the plaster from the base of the plant, and filled in a little earth which I watered every morning. The plant was healthy, and sometimes it produced a small orange marigold.

Sometimes Suraj plucked a flower and kept it in his tray, among the combs, buttons and scent bottles. Sometimes he gave the flower to a passing child, once to a small boy who immediately tore it to shreds. Suraj was back on his rounds, as his exams were over.

Whenever he was tired of going from house to house, Suraj would sit beneath a shady banyan or peepul tree, put his tray aside, and take out his flute. The haunting notes travelled down the road in the afternoon stillness, drawing children to him. They would sit beside him and be very quiet when he played, because there was something melancholic and appealing about the tune. Suraj sometimes made flutes out of pieces of bamboo, but he never sold them. He would give them to the children he liked. He would sell almost anything, but not flutes.

Suraj sometimes played the flute at night, when he lay awake, unable to sleep; but even though I slept, I could hear the music in my dreams. Sometimes he took his flute with him to the crooked tree and played for the benefit of the birds. The parrots made harsh noises in response and flew away. Once, when Suraj was playing his flute to a small group of children, he had a fit. The flute fell from his hands. And he began to roll about in the dust on the roadside. The children became frightened and ran away, but they did not stay away for long. The next time they heard the flute, they came to listen as usual.

XIII

It was Lord Krishna's birthday, and the rain came down as heavily as it is said to have done on the day he was born. Krishna is the best beloved of all the gods. Young mothers laugh or weep as they read or hear the pranks of his boyhood; young men pray to be as tall and as strong as Krishna was when he killed King Kamsa's elephant and wrestlers; young girls dream of a lover as daring as Krishna to carry them off in a war chariot; grown men envy the wisdom and statesmanship with which he managed the affairs of his kingdom.

The rain came so unexpectedly that it took everyone by surprise. In seconds, people were drenched, and within minutes, the streets were flooded. The temple tank overflowed, the railway lines disappeared, and the old wall near the bus stop shivered and silently fell—the sound of its collapse drowned in the downpour. A naked young man with a dancing bear cavorted in the middle of the vegetable market. Pitamber's rickshaw churned through the floodwater while he sang lustily as he worked.

Wading through knee-deep water down the road, I saw the roadside vendors salvaging whatever they could. Plastic toys, cabbages and utensils floated away and were seized by urchins. The water had risen to the level of the shop fronts and the floors were awash. Deep Chand and Ramu, with the help of a customer, were using buckets to bail the water out of their shop. The rain stopped as suddenly as it had begun and the sun came out. The water began to find an outlet, flooding other low-lying areas, and a paper boat came sailing between my legs.

Next morning, the morning on which the result of Suraj's examinations was due, I rose early—the first time I ever got up before Suraj—and went down to the news agency. A small crowd of students had gathered at the bus stop, joking with each other and hiding their nervousness with a show of indifference. There were not many passengers on the first bus, and there was a mad grab for newspapers as the bundle landed with a thud on the pavement. Within half-an-hour, the newsboy had sold all his copies. It was the best day of the year for him.

I went through the columns relating to Pipalnagar, but I couldn't find Suraj's roll number on the list of successful candidates. I had the number on a slip of paper, and I looked at it again to make sure I had compared it correctly with the others; then I went through the newspaper once more. When I returned to the room, Suraj was sitting on the doorstep. I didn't have to tell him he had failed—he knew by the look on my face. I sat down beside him, and we said nothing for some time.

'Never mind,' Suraj said eventually. 'I will pass next time.'

I realized I was more depressed than he was and that he was trying to console me.

'If only you'd had more time,' I said.

'I have a year. And you will have time to finish your book, and then we can go away together. Another year of Pipalnagar won't be so bad. As long as I have your friendship almost everything can be tolerated.'

He stood up, the tray hanging from his shoulders. 'Is there anything you'd like to buy?'

XIV

Another year of Pipalnagar! But it was not to be. A short time later, I received a letter from the editor of a newspaper, calling me to Delhi for an interview. My friends insisted that I should go. Such an opportunity would not come again.

But I needed a shirt. The few I possessed were either frayed at the collar or torn at the shoulders. I hadn't been able to afford a new shirt for over a year, and I couldn't afford one now. Struggling writers weren't expected to dress well, but I felt in order to get the job I would need both a haircut and a clean shirt.

Where was I to go to get a shirt? Suraj generally wore an old red-striped T-shirt; he washed it every second evening, and by morning it was dry and ready to wear again; but it was tight even on him. He did not have another. Besides, I needed something white, something respectable!

I went to Deep Chand who had a collection of shirts. He

was only too glad to lend me one. But they were all brightly coloured—pinks, purples and magentas... No editor was going to be impressed by a young writer in a pink shirt. They looked fine on Deep Chand, but he had no need to look respectable.

Finally, Pitamber came to my rescue. He didn't bother with shirts himself, except in winter, but he was able to borrow a clean white shirt from a guard at the jail, who'd got it from the relative of a convict in exchange for certain favours.

'This shirt will make you look respectable,' said Pitamber. 'To be respectable—what an adventure!'

XV

Freedom. The moment the bus was out of Pipalnagar, and the fields opened out on all sides, I knew that I was free, that I had always been free. Only my own weakness, hesitation, and the habits that had grown around me had held me back. All I had to do was sit in a bus and go somewhere.

I sat near the open window of the bus and let the cool breeze from the fields play against my face. Herons and snipe waded among the lotus roots in flat green ponds. Blue jays swooped around telegraph poles. Children jumped naked into the canals that wound through the fields. Because I was happy, it seemed to me that everyone else was happy—the driver, the conductor, the passengers, the farmers in the fields and those driving bullock carts. When two women behind me started quarrelling over their seats, I helped to placate them. Then I took a small girl on my knee and pointed out camels, buffaloes, vultures and pariah dogs.

Six hours later, the bus crossed the bridge over the swollen Yamuna River, passed under the walls of the great Red Fort built by a Mughal emperor, and entered the old city of Delhi. I found it strange to be in a city again, after several years in

Pipalnagar. It was a little frightening too. I felt like a stranger. No one was interested in me.

In Pipalnagar, people wanted to know each other, or at least to know about one another. In Delhi, no one cared who you were or where you came from, like big cities almost everywhere. It was prosperous but without a heart.

After a day and a night of loneliness, I found myself wishing that Suraj had accompanied me; wishing that I was back in Pipalnagar. But when the job was offered to me—at a starting salary of three hundred rupees per month, a princely sum compared to what I had been making on my own—I did not have the courage to refuse it. After accepting the job—which was to commence in a week's time—I spent the day wandering through the bazaars, down the wide, shady roads of the capital, resting under the jamun trees, and thinking all the time what I would do in the months to come.

I slept at the railway waiting room and all night long I heard the shunting and whistling of engines which conjured up visions of places with sweet names like Kumbakonam, Krishnagiri, Polonnarurawa. I dreamt of palm-fringed beaches and inland lagoons; of the echoing chambers of deserted cities, red sandstone and white marble; of temples in the sun; and elephants crossing wide, slow-moving rivers...

XVI

Pitamber was on the platform when the train steamed into the Pipalnagar station in the early hours of a damp September morning. I waved to him from the carriage window, and shouted that everything had gone well.

But everything was not well here. When I got off the train, Pitamber told me that Suraj had been ill—that he'd had a fit on a lonely stretch of road the previous afternoon and had lain in the sun for over an hour. Pitamber had found him, suffering from heatstroke, and brought him home. When I saw him, he was sitting up on the string bed drinking hot tea. He looked pale and weak, but his smile was reassuring.

'Don't worry,' he said. 'I will be all right.'

'He was bad last night,' said Pitamber. 'He had a fever and kept talking, as in a dream. But what he says is true—he is better this morning.'

'Thanks to Pitamber,' said Suraj. 'It is good to have friends.'

'Come with me to Delhi, Suraj,' I said. 'I have got a job now. You can live with me and attend a school regularly.'

'It is good for friends to help each other,' said Suraj, 'but only after I have passed my exam will I join you in Delhi. I made myself this promise. Poor Pipalnagar—nobody wants to stay here. Will you be sorry to leave?'

'Yes, I will be sorry. A part of me will still be here.'

XVII

Deep Chand was happy to know that I was leaving. 'I'll follow you soon,' he said. 'There is money to be made in Delhi, cutting hair. Girls are keeping it short these days.'

'But men are growing it long.'

'True. So I shall open a barber shop for ladies and a beauty salon for men! Ramu can attend to the ladies.'

Ramu winked at me in the mirror. He was still at the stage of teasing girls on their way to school or college.

The snip of Deep Chand's scissors made me sleepy, as I sat in his chair. His fingers beat a rhythmic tattoo on my scalp. It was my last haircut in Pipalnagar, and Deep Chand did not charge me for it. I promised to write as soon as I had settled down in Delhi.

The next day when Suraj was stronger, I said, 'Come, let

us go for a walk and visit our crooked tree. Where is your flute, Suraj?'

'I don't know. Let us look for it.'

We searched the room and our belongings for the flute but could not find it.

'It must have been left on the roadside,' said Suraj. 'Never mind. I will make another.'

I could picture the flute lying in the dust on the roadside and somehow this made me sad. But Suraj was full of high spirits as we walked across the railway lines and through the fields.

'The rains are over,' he said, kicking off his chappals and lying down on the grass. 'You can smell the autumn in the air. Somehow, it makes me feel light-hearted. Yesterday I was sad, and tomorrow I might be sad again, but today I know that I am happy. I want to live on and on. One lifetime cannot satisfy my heart.'

'A day in a lifetime,' I said. 'I'll remember this day—the way the sun touches us, the way the grass bends, the smell of this leaf as I crush it...'

XVIII

Every morning at six the first bus arrives, and the passengers alight, looking sleepy and dishevelled and rather discouraged by their first sight of Pipalnagar. When they have gone their various ways, the bus is driven into the shed. Cows congregate at the dustbin and the pavement dwellers come to life, stretching their tired limbs on the hard stone steps. I carry the bucket up the steps to my room, and bathe for the last time on the open balcony. In the villages, the buffaloes are wallowing in green ponds while naked urchins sit astride them, scrubbing their backs, and a crow or water bird perches on their glistening necks. The parrots are busy in the crooked tree, and a slim green snake basks in the sun on our island near the brick kiln. In the hills, the mists have lifted and the distant mountains are fringed with snow.

It is autumn, and the rains are over. The earth meets the sky in one broad, bold sweep.

A land of thrusting hills. Terraced hills, wood-covered and windswept. Mountains where the gods speak gently to the lonely. Hills of green grass and grey rock, misty at dawn, hazy at noon, molten at sunset, where fierce, fresh torrents rush to the valleys below. A quiet land of fields and ponds, shaded by ancient trees and ringed with palms, where sacred rivers are touched by temples, where temples are touched by southern seas.

This is the land I should write about. Pipalnagar should be forgotten. I should turn aside from it to sing instead of the splendours of exotic places.

But only yesterdays are truly splendid... And there are other singers, sweeter than I, to sing of tomorrow. I can only write of today, of Pipalnagar, where I have lived and loved.

VOTING AT BARLOWGANJ

I am standing under the deodars, waiting for a taxi. Devilal, one of the candidates in the civic election, is offering free rides to all his supporters, to ensure that they get to the polls in time. I have assured him that I prefer walking but he does not believe me; he fears that I will settle down with a bottle of beer rather than walk the two miles to the Barlowganj polling station to cast my vote. He has gone to the expense of engaging a taxi for the day just to make certain of lingerers like me. He assures me that he is not using unfair means—most of the other candidates are doing the same thing.

It is a cloudy day, promising rain, so I decide I will wait for the taxi. It has been plying since 6 a.m., and now it is ten o'clock. It will continue plying up and down the hill till 4 p.m. and by that time it will have cost Devilal over a hundred rupees.

Here it comes. The driver—like most of our taxi drivers, a Sikh—sees me standing at the gate, screeches to a sudden stop, and opens the door. I am about to get in when I notice that the windscreen carries a sticker displaying the Congress symbol of the cow and calf. Devilal is an Independent, and has adopted a cock bird as his symbol.

'Is this Devilal's taxi?' I ask.

'No, it's the Congress taxi,' says the driver.

'I'm sorry,' I say. 'I don't know the Congress candidate.'

'That's all right,' he says agreeably; he isn't a local man and has no interest in the outcome of the election. 'Devilal's taxi will be along any minute now.'

He moves off, looking for the Congress voters on whose behalf he has been engaged. I am glad that the candidates have had to adopt different symbols; it has saved me the embarrassment of turning up in a Congress taxi, only to vote for an Independent. But the real reason for using symbols is to help illiterate voters know whom they are voting for when it comes to putting their papers in the ballot box. All through the hill station's mini-election campaign, posters have been displaying candidates' symbols—a car, a radio, a cock bird, a tiger, a lamp—and the narrow, winding roads resound to the cries of children who are paid to shout, 'Vote for the Radio!' or 'Vote for the Cock!'

Presently, my taxi arrives. It is already full, having picked up others on the way, and I have to squeeze in at the back with a stout lalain and her bony husband, the local ration-shop owner. Sitting up front, near the driver, is Vinod, a poor, ragged, quite happy-go-lucky youth, who contrives to turn up wherever I happen to be, and frequently involves himself in my activities. He gives me a namaste and a wide grin.

'What are you doing here?' I ask him.

'Same as you, Bond sahib. Voting. Maybe Devilal will give me a job if he wins.'

'But you already have a job. I thought you were the games-boy at the school.'

'That was last month, Bond sahib.'

'They kicked you out?'

'They asked me to leave.'

The taxi gathers speed as it moves smoothly down the winding hill road. The driver is in a hurry; the more trips he makes, the more money he collects. We swerve round sharp corners, and every time the lalain's chubby hands, covered with heavy bangles and rings, clutch at me for support. She and her husband are voting for Devilal because they belong to the same caste; Vinod is voting for him in the hope of getting a job; I am voting for him because I like the man. I find him simple, courteous and ready to listen to complaints about drains, street lighting and wrongly assessed taxes. He even tries to do something about these things. He is a tall, cadaverous man, with paan-stained teeth; no Nixon, Heath or Indira Gandhi; but he knows that Barlowganj folk care little for appearances.

Barlowganj is a small ward (one of four in the hill station of Mussoorie); it has about 1,000 voters. An election campaign has, therefore, to be conducted on a person-to-person basis. There is no point in haranguing a crowd at a street corner; it would be a very small crowd. The only way to canvass support is to visit each voter's house and plead one's cause personally. This means making a lot of promises with a perfectly straight face.

The bazaar and village of Barlowganj crouch in a vale on the way down the mountain to Dehra. The houses on either side of the road are nearly all English-looking, most of them built before the turn of the century. The bazaar is Indian, charming and quite prosperous: tailors sit cross-legged before their sewing machines, turning out blazers and tight trousers for the well-to-do students who attend the many public schools that still thrive here; halwais—potbellied sweet vendors—spend all day sitting on their haunches in front of giant frying pans; and coolies carry huge loads of timber or cement or grain up the steep hill paths.

Who was Barlow, and how did the village get his name? A search through old guides and gazetteers has given me no clue. Perhaps he was a revenue superintendent or a surveyor, who came striding up from the plains in the 1830s to build a hunting lodge in this pleasantly wooded vale. That was how most hill stations began. The police station, the little Church of the Resurrection, and the ruined brewery were among the earliest buildings in Barlowganj.

The brewery is a mound of rubble, but the road that came into existence to serve the needs of the old Crown Brewery is the one that now serves our taxi. Buckle and Co.'s 'Bullock Train' was the chief means of transport in the old days. Mr Bohle, one of the pioneers of brewing in India, started the 'Old Brewery' at Mussoorie in 1830. Two years later, he got into trouble with the authorities for supplying beer to soldiers without permission; he had to move elsewhere.

But the great days of the brewery business really began in 1876, when everyone suddenly acclaimed a much-improved brew. The source was traced to Vat 42 in Whymper's Crown Brewery (the one whose ruins we are now passing), and the beer was retasted and retested until the diminishing level of the barrel revealed the perfectly brewed remains of a soldier who had been reported missing some months previously. He had evidently fallen into the vat and been drowned and, unknown to himself, had given the Barlowganj beer trade a real fillip. Apocryphal though this story may sound, I have it on the authority of the owner of the now defunct Mafasalite Press who, in a short account of Mussoorie, wrote that 'meat was thereafter recognized as the missing component and was scrupulously added till more modern, and less cannibalistic, means were discovered to satiate the froth-blower'.

Recently, confirmation came from an old India hand now living in London. He wrote to me reminiscing of early days in the hill station and had this to say:

> Uncle Georgie Forster was working for the Crown Brewery when a coolie fell in. Coolies were employed to remove

> scum etc. from the vats. They walked along planks suspended over the vats. Poor devil must have slipped and fallen in. Uncle often told us about the incident and there was no doubt that the beer tasted very good.

What with soldiers and coolies falling into the vats with seeming regularity, one wonders whether there may have been more to these accidents than meets the eye. I have a nagging suspicion that Whymper and Buckle may have been the Burke and Hare of Mussoorie's beer industry.

But no beer is made in Mussoorie today, and Devilal probably regrets the passing of the breweries as much as I do. Only the walls of the breweries remain, and these are several feet thick. The roofs and girders must have been removed for use in other buildings. Moss and sorrel grow in the old walls, and wildcats live in dark corners protected from rain and wind.

We have taken the sharpest curves and steepest gradients, and now our taxi moves smoothly along a fairly level road which might pass for a country lane in England were it not for the clumps of bamboo on either side.

A mist has come up the valley to settle over Barlowganj, and out of the mist looms an imposing mansion, Sikander Hall, which is still owned and occupied by the Skinners, descendants of Colonel James Skinner who raised a body of Irregular Horse for the Marathas. This was absorbed by the East India Company's forces in 1803. The cavalry regiment is still known as Skinner's Horse, but of course it is a tank regiment now. Skinner's troops called him 'Sikander' (a corruption of both Skinner and Alexander), and that is the name his property bears. The Skinners who live here now have, quite sensibly, gone in for keeping pigs and poultry.

The next house belongs to the Raja of K but he is unable

to maintain it on his diminishing privy purse, and it has been rented out as an ashram for members of a saffron-robed sect who would rather meditate in the hills than in the plains. There was a time when it was only the sahibs and rajas who could afford to spend the entire 'season' in Mussoorie. The new rich are the industrialists and maharishis. The coolies and rickshaw pullers are no better off than when I was a boy in Mussoorie. They still carry or pull the same heavy loads, for the same pittance, and seldom attain the age of forty. Only their clientele has changed.

One more gate, and here is Colonel Powell in his khaki bush shirt and trousers, a uniform that never varies with the seasons. He is an old shikari; once wrote a book called *The Call of the Tiger.* He is too old for hunting now, but likes to yarn with me when we meet on the road. His wife has gone home to England, but he does not want to leave India.

'It's the mountains,' he was telling me the other day. 'Once the mountains are in your blood, there is no escape. You have to come back again and again. I don't think I'd like to die anywhere else.'

Today there is no time to stop and chat. The taxi driver, with a vigorous blowing of his horn, takes the car round the last bend, and then through the village and narrow bazaar of Barlowganj, stopping about a hundred yards from the polling stations.

There is a festive air about Barlowganj today, I have never seen so many people in the bazaar. Bunting, in the form of rival posters and leaflets, is strung across the street. The tea shops are doing a roaring trade. There is much last-minute canvassing, and I have to run the gamut of various candidates and their agents. For the first time, I learn the names of some of the candidates. In all, seven men are competing for this seat.

A schoolboy, smartly dressed and speaking English, is the first to accost me. He says: 'Don't vote for Devilal, sir. He's a big crook. Vote for Jatinder! See, sir, that's his symbol—the bow and arrow.'

'I shall certainly think about the bow and arrow,' I tell him politely.

Another agent, a man, approaches, and says, 'I hope you are going to vote for the Congress candidate.'

'I don't know anything about him,' I say.

'That doesn't matter. It's the party you are voting for. Don't forget it's Mrs Gandhi's party.'

Meanwhile, one of Devilal's lieutenants has been keeping a close watch on both Vinod and me, to make sure that we are not seduced by rival propaganda. I give the man a reassuring smile and stride purposefully towards the polling station, which has been set up in the municipal schoolhouse. Policemen stand at the entrance, to make sure that no one approaches the voters once they have entered the precincts.

I join the patient queue of voters. Everyone is in good humour, and there is no breaking of the line; these are not film stars we have come to see. Vinod is in another line, and grins proudly at me across the passageway. This is the one day in his life on which he has been made to feel really important. And he *is*. In a small constituency like Barlowganj, every vote counts.

Most of my fellow voters are poor people. Local issues mean something to them, affect their daily living. The more affluent can buy their way out of trouble, can pay for small conveniences; few of them bother to come to the polls. But for the 'common man'—the shopkeeper, clerk, teacher, domestic servant, milkman, mule driver—this is a big day. The man he is voting for has promised him something, and the voter means to take the successful candidate up on his promise. Not for another five years will the same fuss be made over the local cobblers, tailors and laundrymen. Their votes are indeed precious.

And now it is my turn to vote. I confirm my name, address and roll number. I am down on the list as 'Rusking Bound', but I let it pass: I might forfeit my right to vote if I raise any objection at this stage! A dab of marking-ink is placed on my forefinger—this is so that I do not come round a second time—and I am given a paper displaying the names and symbols of all the candidates. I am then directed to the privacy of a small booth, where I place the official rubber stamp against Devilal's name. This done, I fold the paper in four and slip it into the ballot box.

All has gone smoothly. Vinod is waiting for me outside. So is Devilal.

'Did you vote for me?' asks Devilal.

It is my eyes that he is looking at, not my lips, when I reply in the affirmative. He is a shrewd man, with many years' experience in seeing through bluff. He is pleased with my reply, beams at me, and directs me to the waiting taxi.

Vinod and I get in together, and soon we are on the road again, being driven swiftly homewards up the winding hill road.

Vinod is looking pleased with himself; rather smug, in fact. 'You did vote for Devilal?' I ask him. 'The symbol of the cock bird?'

He shakes his head, keeping his eyes on the road. 'No, the cow,' he says.

'You ass!' I exclaim. 'Devilal's symbol was the cock, not the cow!'

'I know,' he says, 'but I like the cow better.'*

I subside into silence. It is a good thing no one else in the taxi has been paying any attention to our conversation. It would

*In spite of Vinod's defection, Devilal won in 1974

be a pity to see Vinod turned out of Devilal's taxi and made to walk the remaining mile to the top of the hill. After all, it will be another five years before he gets another free taxi ride.

A MAGIC OIL

A day or two later I was in the bank, run by Vishaal (manager), Negi (cashier), and Suresh (peon). I was sitting opposite Vishaal, who was at his desk, taken up by two handsome paperweights but no papers. Suresh had brought me a cup of tea from the tea shop across the road. There was just one customer in the bank, Hassan, who was making a deposit. A cosy summer morning in Fosterganj: not much happening, but life going on just the same.

In walked Foster. He'd made an attempt at shaving, but appeared to have given up at a crucial stage, because now he looked like a wasted cricketer finally on his way out. The effect was enhanced by the fact that he was wearing flannel trousers that had once been white but were now greenish yellow; the previous monsoon was to blame. He had found an old tie, and this was strung round his neck, or rather his unbuttoned shirt collar. The said shirt had seen many summers and winters in Fosterganj, and was frayed at the cuffs. Even so, Foster looked quite spry, as compared to when I had last seen him.

'Come in, come in!' said Vishaal, always polite to his customers, even those who had no savings. 'How is your gladioli farm?'

'Coming up nicely,' said Foster. 'I'm growing potatoes too.'

'Very nice. But watch out for the porcupines, they love potatoes.'

'Shot one last night. Cut my hands getting the quills out. But porcupine meat is great. I'll send you some the next time I shoot one.'

'Well, keep some ammunition for the leopard. We've got to get it before it kills someone else.'

'It won't be around for two or three weeks. They keep moving, those leopards. He'll circle the mountain, then be back in these parts. But that's not what I came to see you about, Mr Vishaal. I was hoping for a small loan.'

'Small loan, big loan, that's what we are here for. In what way can we help you, sir?'

'I want to start a chicken farm.'

'Most original.'

'There's a great shortage of eggs in Mussoorie. The hotels want eggs, the schools want eggs, the restaurants want eggs. And they have to get them from Rajpur or Dehradun.'

'Hassan has a few hens,' I put in.

'Only enough for home consumption. I'm thinking in terms of hundreds of eggs—and broiler chickens for the table. I want to make Fosterganj the chicken capital of India. It will be like old times, when my ancestor planted the first potatoes here, brought all the way from Scotland!'

'I thought they came from Ireland,' I said. 'Captain Young, up at Landour.'

'Oh well, we brought other things. Like Scotch whisky.'

'Actually, Irish whisky got here first. Captain Kennedy, up in Shimla.' I wasn't Irish, but I was in a combative frame of mind, which is the same as being Irish.

To mollify Foster, I said, 'You did bring the bagpipe.' And when he perked up, I added: 'But the Gurkha is better at playing it.'

This contretemps over, Vishaal got Foster to sign a couple

of forms and told him that the loan would be processed in due course and that we'd all celebrate over a bottle of Scotch whisky. Foster left the room with something of a swagger. The prospect of some money coming in—even if it is someone else's—will put any man in an optimistic frame of mind. And for Foster the prospect of losing it was as yet far distant.

I wanted to make a phone call to my bank in Delhi, so that I could have some of my savings sent to me, and Vishaal kindly allowed me to use his phone.

There were only four phones in all of Fosterganj, and there didn't seem to be any necessity for more. The bank had one. So did Dr Bisht. So did Brigadier Bakshi, retired. And there was one in the police station, but it was usually out of order.

The police station, a one-room affair, was manned by a Daroga and a constable. If the Daroga felt like a nap, the constable took charge. And if the constable took the afternoon off, the Daroga would run the place. This worked quite well, as there wasn't much crime in Fosterganj—if you didn't count Foster's illicit still at the bottom of the hill (Scottish hooch, he called the stuff he distilled); or a charming young delinquent called Sunil, who picked pockets for a living (though not in Fosterganj); or the barber who supplemented his income by supplying charas to his agents at some of the boarding schools; or the man who sold the secretions of certain lizards, said to increase sexual potency—except that it was only linseed oil, used for oiling cricket bats.

I found the last mentioned, a man called Rattan Lal, sitting on a stool outside my door when I returned from the bank.

'*Saande-ka-tel*,' he declared abruptly, holding up a small bottle containing a vitreous yellow fluid. 'Just one application, Sahib, and the size and strength of your valuable member will increase dramatically. It will break down doors, should doors be shut against you. No chains will hold it down. You will be like a stallion, rampant in a field full of fillies. Sahib, you will rule the roost! Memsahibs and beautiful women will fall at your feet.'

'It will get me into trouble, for certain,' I demurred. 'It's great stuff, I'm sure. But wasted here in Fosterganj.'

Rattan Lal would not be deterred. 'Sahib, every time you try it, you will notice an increase in dimensions, guaranteed!'

'Like Pinocchio's nose,' I said in English. He looked puzzled. He understood the word 'nose', but had no idea what I meant.

'Naak?' he said. 'No, Sahib, you don't rub it on your nose. Here, down between the legs,' and he made as if to give a demonstration. I held a hand up to restrain him.

'There was a boy named Pinocchio in a far-off country,' I explained, switching back to Hindi. 'His nose grew longer every time he told a lie.'

'I tell no lies, Sahib. Look, my nose is normal. Rest is very big. You want to see?'

'Another day,' I said.

'Only ten rupees.'

'The bottle or the rest of you?'

'You joke, Sahib,' and he thrust a bottle into my unwilling hands and removed a ten rupee note from my shirt pocket; all done very simply.

'I will come after a month and check up,' he said. 'Next time I will bring the saanda itself! You are in the prime of your life, it will make you a bull among men.' And away he went.

◆

The little bottle of oil stood unopened on the bathroom shelf for weeks. I was too scared to use it. It was like the bottle in Alice in Wonderland with the label DRINK ME. Alice drank it, and shot up to the ceiling. I wasn't sure I wanted to grow that high.

I did wonder what would happen if I applied some of it to my scalp. Would it stimulate hair growth? Would it stimulate my thought processes? Put an end to writer's block?

Well, I never did find out. One afternoon I heard a clatter in the bathroom and looked in to see a large and sheepish looking monkey jump out of the window with the bottle.

But to return to Rattan Lal—some hours after I had been sold the aphrodisiac, I was walking up to town to get a newspaper when I met him on his way down.

'Any luck with the magic oil?' I asked.

'All sold out!' he said, beaming with pleasure. 'Ten bottles sold at the Savoy, and six at Hakman's. What a night it's going to be for them.' And he rubbed his hands at the prospect.

'A very busy night,' I said. 'Either that, or they'll be looking for you to get their money back.'

'I will come next month. If you are still here, I'll keep another bottle for you. Look there!' He took me by the arm and pointed at a large rock lizard that was sunning itself on the parapet. 'You catch me some of those, and I'll pay you for them. Be my partner. Bring me lizards—not small ones, only big fellows—and I will buy!'

'How do you extract the tel?' I asked.

'Ah, that's a trade secret. But I will show you when you bring me some saandas. Now I must go. My good wife waits for me with impatience.'

And off he went, down the bridle path to Rajpur.

The rock lizard was still on the wall, enjoying its afternoon siesta.

It did occur to me that I might make a living from breeding rock lizards. Perhaps Vishaal would give me a loan. I wasn't making much as a writer.

THE HORSESHOE

'What's this?' asked Rakesh, when he was a small boy, touching the huge horseshoe that stood on my desk.

'It's a horseshoe,' I said, 'I keep it for luck.'

'But it's so big! It must have been a very big horse. Like a dinosaur!'

'Not a dinosaur, but an English carthorse. They are not very tall, but they are sturdy animals, used to pull carts and ploughs. And they have big feet. This is a carthorse's shoe. About four times bigger than the shoes of the little hill ponies we see in Mussoorie.'

'Are there any carthorses in India?'

'Not as far as I know. You'll find them on farms in England or France.'

'Then how did you get it, Dada?'

'Miss Bean gave it to me.'

And then I told him about Miss Bean, the old English lady who had grown up in Mussoorie, and who lived in Maplewood Cottage when I came to live there in 1963.

Yes, it's exactly fifty years since I came to live in the hill station, renting the little cottage that stood on its own on the edge of a maple and oak forest. Rakesh wasn't born then.

Miss Bean was in her eighties, the 'last surviving Bean' as she described herself. Her parents, brother and sister were all buried in the Camel's Back Cemetery. She received a tiny pension and lived in a small room full of bric-a-brac, bits of furniture rescued from her old home, and paintings done by her late mother. I was on my own then, living on sardines, baked beans and other tinned stuff. Sometimes I shared my simple meals with her.

She told me stories of Mussoorie's early days—the balls and fancy dress parties at Hakman's and the Savoy; the scandals that erupted from time to time; houses that were said to be haunted; friends who had gone away or gone to their Maker; her father's military exploits.

I had noticed the big horseshoe on the mantelpiece, and asked her how she came by it. 'My father brought it out from England,' she said. 'It was supposed to bring us luck. But the good luck ran out long ago... You can have it, if you like it.' And she presented me with the horseshoe.

Well, it's been with me all these years, going almost unnoticed most of the time, except when a visitor notices it and comments on its size.

Miss Bean passed away in her sleep, while I was still at Maplewood. Prem came to work for me, and brought his wife and three-month old Rakesh from the village to live with us. They stayed for the rest of my long sojourn in the hills.

Rakesh is now forty. He and his pretty wife Beena have three school-going children. The horseshoe is still reclining on my desk.

Beena was asking me about it this morning. 'Did it really bring you good luck?'

'We make our own luck,' I said. 'But that horseshoe has been with us all these years, and it always reminds me of its former owner, a little old lady who didn't have much luck, but who enjoyed living and stood alone, without complaining. It's courage, not luck that takes us through to the end of the road.'

THE ROOM OF MANY COLOURS

Last week I wrote a story, and all the time I was writing it I thought it was a good story; but when it was finished and I had read it through, I found that there was something missing, that it didn't ring true. So I tore it up. I wrote a poem, about an old man sleeping in the sun, and this was true, but it was finished quickly, and once again I was left with the problem of what to write next. And I remembered my father, who taught me to write; and I thought, why not write about my father, and about the trees we planted, and about the people I knew while growing up and about what happened on the way to growing up…

And so, like Alice, I must begin at the beginning, and in the beginning there was this red insect, just like a velvet button, which I found on the front lawn of the bungalow. The grass was still wet with overnight rain.

I placed the insect on the palm of my hand and took it into the house to show my father.

'Look, Dad,' I said, 'I haven't seen an insect like this before. Where has it come from?'

'Where did you find it?' he asked.

'On the grass.'

'It must have come down from the sky,' he said. 'It must have come down with the rain.'

Later he told me how the insect really happened but I

preferred his first explanation. It was more fun to have it dropping from the sky.

I was seven at the time, and my father was thirty-seven, but, right from the beginning, he made me feel that I was old enough to talk to him about everything—insects, people, trees, steam engines, King George, comics, crocodiles, the Mahatma, the Viceroy, America, Mozambique and Timbuctoo. We took long walks together, explored old ruins, chased butterflies and waved to passing trains.

My mother had gone away when I was four, and I had very dim memories of her. Most other children had their mothers with them, and I found it a bit strange that mine couldn't stay. Whenever I asked my father why she'd gone, he'd say, 'You'll understand when you grow up.' And if I asked him *where* she had gone, he'd look troubled and say, 'I really don't know.' This was the only question of mine to which he didn't have an answer.

But I was quite happy living alone with my father; I had never known any other kind of life.

We were sitting on an old wall, looking out to sea at a couple of Arab dhows and a tram steamer, when my father said, 'Would you like to go to sea one day?'

'Where does the sea go?' I asked.

'It goes everywhere.'

'Does it go to the end of the world?'

'It goes right round the world. It's a round world.'

'It can't be.'

'It is. But it's so big, you can't see the roundness. When a fly sits on a watermelon, it can't see right round the melon, can it? The melon must seem quite flat to the fly. Well, in comparison to the world, we're much, much smaller than the tiniest of insects.'

'Have you been around the world?' I asked.

'No, only as far as England. That's where your grandfather was born.'

'And my grandmother?'

'She came to India from Norway when she was quite small. Norway is a cold land, with mountains and snow, and the sea cutting deep into the land. I was there as a boy. It's very beautiful, and the people are good and work hard.'

'I'd like to go there.'

'You will, one day. When you are older, I'll take you to Norway.'

'Is it better than England?'

'It's quite different.'

'Is it better than India?'

'It's quite different.'

'Is India like England?'

'No, it's different.'

'Well, what does "different" mean?'

'It means things are not the same. It means people are different. It means the weather is different. It means trees and birds and insects are different.'

'Are English crocodiles different from Indian crocodiles?'

'They don't have crocodiles in England.'

'Oh, then it must be different.'

'It would be a dull world if it was the same everywhere,' said my father.

He never lost patience with my endless questioning. If he wanted a rest, he would take out his pipe and spend a long time lighting it. If this took very long I'd find something else to do. But sometimes I'd wait patiently until the pipe was drawing, and then return to the attack.

'Will we always be in India?' I asked.

'No, we'll have to go away one day. You see, it's hard to

explain, but it isn't really our country.'

'Ayah says it belongs to the king of England, and the jewels in his crown were taken from India, and that when the Indians get their jewels back the king will lose India! But first they have to get the crown from the king, but this is very difficult, she says, because the crown is always on his head. He even sleeps wearing his crown!'

Ayah was my nanny. She loved me deeply, and was always filling my head with strange and wonderful stories.

My father did not comment on Ayah's views. All he said was, 'We'll have to go away some day.'

'How long have we been here?' I asked.

'Two hundred years.'

'No, I mean us.'

'Well, you were born in India, so that's seven years for you.'

'Then can't I stay here?'

'Do you want to?'

'I want to go across the sea. But can we take Ayah with us?'

'I don't know, son. Let's walk along the beach.'

We lived in an old palace beside a lake. The palace looked like a ruin from the outside, but the rooms were cool and comfortable. We lived in one wing, and my father organized a small school in another wing. His pupils were the children of the raja and the raja's relatives. My father had started life in India as a tea planter, but he had been trained as a teacher and the idea of starting a school in a small state facing the Arabian Sea had appealed to him. The pay wasn't much, but we had a palace to live in, the latest 1938 model Hillman to drive about in, and a number of servants. In those days, of course, everyone had servants (although the servants did not have any!). Ayah was our own; but the cook, the bearer, the gardener and the bhisti were all provided by the state.

Sometimes I sat in the schoolroom with the other children (who were all much bigger than me), sometimes I remained in the house with Ayah, sometimes I followed the gardener, Dukhi, about the spacious garden.

Dukhi means 'sad', and though I never could discover if the gardener had anything to feel sad about, the name certainly suited him. He had grown to resemble the drooping weeds that he was always digging up with a tiny spade. I seldom saw him standing up. He always sat on the ground with his knees well up to his chin, and attacked the weeds from this position. He could spend all day on his haunches, moving about the garden simply by shuffling his feet along the grass.

I tried to imitate his posture, sitting down on my heels and putting my knees into my armpits, but I could never hold the position for more than five minutes.

Time had no meaning in a large garden, and Dukhi never hurried. Life, for him, was not a matter of one year succeeding another, but of five seasons—winter, spring, hot weather, monsoon and autumn—arriving and departing. His seedbeds always had to be in readiness for the coming season, and he did not look any further than the next monsoon. It was impossible to tell his age. He may have been thirty-six or eighty-six. He was either very young for his years or very old for them.

Dukhi loved bright colours, especially reds and yellows. He liked strongly scented flowers, like jasmine and honeysuckle. He couldn't understand my father's preference for the more delicately perfumed petunias and sweetpeas. But I shared Dukhi's fondness for the common bright orange marigold, which is offered in temples and is used to make garlands and nosegays. When the garden was bare of all colour, the marigold would still be there, gay and flashy, challenging the sun.

Dukhi was very fond of making nosegays, and I liked to

watch him at work. A sunflower formed the centrepiece. It was surrounded by roses, marigolds and oleander, fringed with green leaves and bound together with silver thread. The perfume was overpowering. The nosegays were presented to me or my father on special occasions, that is, on a birthday or to guests of my father's who were considered important.

One day I found Dukhi making a nosegay, and said, 'No one is coming today, Dukhi. It isn't even a birthday.'

'It is a birthday, Chota Sahib,' he said. 'Little Sahib' was the title he had given me. It wasn't much of a title compared to Raja Sahib, Diwan Sahib or Burra Sahib, but it was nice to have a title at the age of seven.

'Oh,' I said. 'And is there a party, too?'

'No party.'

'What's the use of a birthday without a party? What's the use of a birthday without presents?'

'This person doesn't like presents—just flowers.'

'Who is it?' I asked, full of curiosity.

'If you want to find out, you can take these flowers to her. She lives right at the top of that far side of the palace. There are twenty-two steps to climb. Remember that, Chota Sahib, you take twenty-three steps and you will go over the edge and into the lake!'

I started climbing the stairs.

It was a spiral staircase of wrought iron, and it went round and round and up and up, and it made me quite dizzy and tired.

At the top I found myself on a small balcony, which looked out over the lake and another palace, at the crowded city and the distant harbour. I heard a voice, a rather high, musical voice, saying (in English), 'Are you a ghost?' I turned to see who had spoken but found the balcony empty. The voice had come from a dark room.

I turned to the stairway, ready to flee, but the voice said, 'Oh, don't go, there's nothing to be frightened of!'

And so I stood still, peering cautiously into the darkness of the room.

'First, tell me—are you a ghost?'

'I'm a boy,' I said.

'And I'm a girl. We can be friends. I can't come out there, so you had better come in. Come along, I'm not a ghost either—not yet, anyway!'

As there was nothing very frightening about the voice, I stepped into the room. It was dark inside, and coming in from the glare, it took me some time to make out the tiny, elderly lady seated on a cushioned gilt chair. She wore a red sari, lots of coloured bangles on her wrists and golden earrings. Her hair was streaked with white, but her skin was still quite smooth and unlined, and she had large and very beautiful eyes.

'You must be Master Bond!' she said. 'Do you know who I am?'

'You're a lady with a birthday,' I said, 'but that's all I know. Dukhi didn't tell me any more.'

'If you promise to keep it a secret, I'll tell you who I am. You see, everyone thinks I'm mad. Do you think so too?'

'I don't know.'

'Well, you must tell me if you think so,' she said with a chuckle. Her laugh was the sort of sound made by the gecko, a little wall lizard, coming from deep down in the throat. 'I have a feeling you are a truthful boy. Do you find it very difficult to tell the truth?'

'Sometimes.'

'Sometimes. Of course, there are times when I tell lies—lots of little lies—because they're such fun! But would you call me a liar? I wouldn't, if I were you, but *would* you?'

'Are you a liar?'

'I'm asking you! If I were to tell you that I was a queen—that I *am* a queen—would you believe me?'

I thought deeply about this, and then said, 'I'll try to believe you.'

'Oh, but you *must* believe me. I'm a real queen, I'm a rani! Look, I've got diamonds to prove it!' And she held out her hands and there was a ring on each finger, the stones glowing and glittering in the dim light. 'Diamonds, rubies, pearls and emeralds! Only a queen can have these!' She was most anxious that I should believe her.

'You must be a queen,' I said.

'Right!' she snapped. 'In that case, would you mind calling me "Your Highness"?'

'Your Highness,' I said.

She smiled. It was a slow, beautiful smile. Her whole face lit up.

'I could love you,' she said. 'But better still, I'll give you something to eat. Do you like chocolates?'

'Yes, Your Highness.'

'Well,' she said, taking a box from the table beside her, 'these have come all the way from England. Take two. Only two, mind, otherwise the box will finish before Thursday, and I don't want that to happen because I won't get any more till Saturday. That's when Captain MacWhirr's ship gets in, the *SS Lucy*, loaded with boxes and boxes of chocolates!'

'All for you?' I asked in considerable awe.

'Yes, of course. They have to last at least three months. I get them from England. I get only the best chocolates. I like them with pink crunchy fillings, don't you?'

'Oh, yes!' I exclaimed, full of envy.

'Never mind,' she said, 'I may give you one, now and then—

if you're very nice to me! Here you are, help yourself…' She pushed the chocolate box towards me.

I took a silver-wrapped chocolate, and then just as I was thinking of taking a second, she quickly took the box away.

'No more!' she said. 'They have to last till Saturday.'

'But I took only *one*,' I said with some indignation.

'Did you?' She gave me a sharp look, decided I was telling the truth, and said graciously, 'Well, in that case you can have another.'

Watching the rani carefully, in case she snatched the box away again, I selected a second chocolate, this one with a green wrapper. I don't remember what kind of day it was outside, but I remember the bright green of the chocolate wrapper.

I thought it would be rude to eat the chocolates in front of a queen, so I put them in my pocket and said, 'I'd better go now. Ayah will be looking for me.'

'And when will you be coming to see me again?'

'I don't know,' I said.

'There's something I want you to do for me,' she said, placing one finger on my shoulder and giving me a conspiratorial look. 'Will you do it?'

'What is it, Your Highness?'

'What is it? Why do you ask? A real prince never asks where or why or whatever, he simply does what the princess asks of him. When I was a princess—before I became a queen, that is—I asked a prince to swim across the lake and fetch me a lily growing on the other bank.'

'And did he get it for you?'

'He drowned halfway across. Let that be a lesson to you. Never agree to do something without knowing what it is.'

'But I thought you said...'

'Never mind what I said. It's what I say that matters!'

'Oh, all right,' I said, fidgeting to be gone. 'What is it you want me to do?'

'Nothing.' Her tiny rosebud lips pouted and she stared sullenly at a picture on the wall. Now that my eyes had grown used to the dim light in the room, I noticed that the walls were hung with portraits of stout rajas and ranis, turbaned and bedecked in fine clothes. There were also portraits of Queen Victoria and King George V of England. And, in the centre of all this distinguished company, a large picture of Mickey Mouse.

'I'll do it if it isn't too dangerous,' I said.

'Then listen.' She took my hand and drew me towards her—what a tiny hand she had!—and whispered, 'I want a *red* rose from the palace garden. But be careful! Don't let Dukhi the gardener catch you. He'll know it's for me. He knows I love roses. And he hates me! I'll tell you why, one day. But if he catches you, he'll do something terrible.'

'To me?'

'No, to himself. That's much worse, isn't it? He'll tie himself into knots, or lie naked on a bed of thorns, or go on a long fast with nothing to eat but fruit, sweets and chicken! So you will be careful, won't you?'

'Oh, but he doesn't hate you,' I cried in protest, remembering the flowers he'd sent for her, and looking around I found that I'd been sitting on them. 'Look, he sent these flowers for your birthday!'

'Well, if he sent them for my birthday, you can take them back,' she snapped. 'But if he sent them for *me*...' and she suddenly softened and looked coy, 'then I might keep them. Thank you, my dear, it was a very sweet thought.' And she leaned forward as though to kiss me.

'It's late, I must go!' I said in alarm, and turning on my heels, ran out of the room and down the spiral staircase.

Father hadn't started lunch, or rather tiffin, as we called it then. He usually waited for me if I was late. I don't suppose he enjoyed eating alone.

For tiffin we usually had rice, mutton curry (koftas or meat balls, with plenty of gravy, was my favourite curry), fried dal and a hot lime or mango pickle. For supper, we had English food—a soup, roast pork and fried potatoes, a rich gravy made by my father, and a custard or caramel pudding. My father enjoyed cooking, but it was only in the morning that he found time for it. Breakfast was his own creation. He cooked eggs in a variety of interesting ways, and favoured some Italian recipes which he had collected during a trip to Europe, long before I was born.

In deference to the feelings of our Hindu friends, we did not eat beef, but, apart from mutton and chicken, there was a plentiful supply of other meats—partridge, venison, lobster and even porcupine!

'And where have you been?' asked my father, helping himself to rice as soon as he saw me come in.

'To the top of the old palace,' I said.

'Did you meet anyone there?'

'Yes, I met a tiny lady who told me she was a rani. She gave me chocolates.'

'As a rule, she doesn't like visitors.'

'Oh, she didn't mind me. But is she really a queen?'

'Well, she's the daughter of a maharaja. That makes her a princess. She never married. There's a story that she fell in love with a commoner, one of the palace servants, and wanted to marry him, but of course they wouldn't allow that. She became very melancholic, and started living all by herself in the old palace. They give her everything she needs, but she doesn't go out or have visitors. Everyone says she's mad.'

'How do they know?' I asked.

'Because she's different from other people, I suppose.'

'Is that being mad?'

'No. Not really, I suppose madness is not seeing things as others see them.'

'Is that very bad?'

'No,' said Father, who for once was finding it very difficult to explain something to me. 'But people who are like that—people whose minds are so different that they don't think, step by step, as we do, whose thoughts jump all over the place—such people are very difficult to live with…'

'Step by step,' I repeated. 'Step by step…'

'You aren't eating,' said my father. 'Hurry up, and you can come with me to school today.'

I always looked forward to attending my father's classes. He did not take me to the schoolroom very often, because he wanted school to be a treat, to begin with, and then later, the routine wouldn't be so unwelcome.

Sitting there with older children, understanding only half of what they were learning, I felt important and part grown-up. And of course I did learn to read and write, although I first learnt to read upside-down, by means of standing in front of the others' desks and peering across at their books. Later, when I went to school, I had some difficulty in learning to read the right way up; and even today I sometimes read upside-down, for the sake of variety. I don't mean that I read standing on my head, simply that I held the book upside-down.

I had at my command a number of rhymes and jingles, the most interesting of these being 'Solomon Grundy'.

Solomon Grundy,
Born on a Monday,
Christened on Tuesday,

Married on Wednesday,
Took ill on Thursday,
Worse on Friday,
Died on Saturday,
Buried on Sunday:
This is the end of
Solomon Grundy.

Was that all that life amounted to, in the end? And were we all Solomon Grundys? These were questions that bothered me at the time. Another puzzling rhyme was the one that went:

Hark, hark,
The dogs do bark,
The beggars are coming to town;
Some in rags,
Some in bags,
And some in velvet gowns.

This rhyme puzzled me for a long time. There were beggars aplenty in the bazaar, and sometimes they came to the house, and some of them did wear rags and bags (and some nothing at all) and the dogs did bark at them, but the beggar in the velvet gown never came our way.

'Who's this beggar in a velvet gown?'

I asked my father. 'Not a beggar at all,' he said.

'Then why call him one?'

And I went to Ayah and asked her the same question, 'Who is the beggar in the velvet gown?'

'Jesus Christ,' said Ayah.

Ayah was a fervent Christian and made me say my prayers at night, even when I was very sleepy. She had, I think, Arab and Negro blood in addition to the blood of the Koli fishing community to which her mother had belonged. Her father, a sailor on an Arab dhow, had been a convert to Christianity. Ayah was a large, buxom woman, with heavy hands and feet and a slow, swaying gait that had all the grace and majesty of a royal elephant. Elephants for all their size are nimble creatures; and Ayah, too, was nimble, sensitive and gentle with her big hands. Her face was always sweet and childlike.

Although a Christian, she clung to many of the beliefs of her parents and loved to tell me stories about mischievous spirits and evil spirits, humans who changed into animals, and snakes who had been princes in their former lives.

There was the story of the snake who married a princess. At first the princess did not wish to marry the snake, whom she had met in a forest, but the snake insisted saying, 'I'll kill you if you won't marry me,' and of course that settled the question. The snake led his bride away and took her to a great treasure. 'I was a prince in my former life,' he explained. 'This treasure is yours.' And then the snake very gallantly disappeared.

'Snakes,' declared Ayah, 'were very lucky omens if seen early in the morning.'

'But, what if the snake bites the lucky person?' I asked.

'He will be lucky all the same,' said Ayah with a logic that was all her own.

Snakes! There were a number of them living in the big garden, and my father had advised me to avoid the long grass. But I had seen snakes crossing the road (a lucky omen, according to Ayah) and they were never aggressive.

'A snake won't attack you,' said Father, 'provided you leave it alone. Of course, if you step on one it will probably bite.'

'Are all snakes poisonous?'

'Yes, but only a few are poisonous enough to kill a man. Others use their poison on rats and frogs. A good thing, too, otherwise during the rains the house would be taken over by the frogs.'

One afternoon, while Father was at school, Ayah found a snake in the bathtub. It wasn't early morning and so the snake couldn't have been a lucky one. Ayah was frightened and ran into the garden calling for help. Dukhi came running. Ayah ordered me to stay outside while they went after the snake.

And it was while I was alone in the garden—an unusual circumstance, since Dukhi was nearly always there—that I remembered the rani's request. On an impulse, I went to the nearest rose bush and plucked the largest rose, pricking my thumb in the process.

And then, without waiting to see what had happened to the snake (it finally escaped), I started up the steps to the top of the old palace.

When I got to the top, I knocked on the door of the rani's room. Getting no reply, I walked along the balcony until I reached another doorway. There were wooden panels around the door, with elephants, camels and turbaned warriors carved into it. As the door was open, I walked boldly into the room then stood still in astonishment. The room was filled with a strange light.

There were windows going right round the room, and each small windowpane was made of a different coloured glass. The sun that came through one window flung red and green and purple colours on the figure of the little rani who stood there with her face pressed to the glass.

She spoke to me without turning from the window. 'This is my favourite room. I have all the colours here. I can see a different world through each pane of glass. Come, join me!' And she beckoned to me, her small hand fluttering like a delicate butterfly.

I went up to the rani. She was only a little taller than me, and we were able to share the same windowpane.

'See, it's a red world!' she said.

The garden below, the palace and the lake, were all tinted red. I watched the rani's world for a little while and then touched her on the arm and said, 'I have brought you a rose!'

She started away from me, and her eyes looked frightened. She would not look at the rose.

'Oh, why did you bring it?' she cried, wringing her hands. 'He'll be arrested now!'

'Who'll be arrested?'

'The prince, of course!'

'But *I* took it,' I said. 'No one saw me. Ayah and Dukhi were inside the house, catching a snake.'

'Did they catch it?' she asked, forgetting about the rose.

'I don't know. I didn't wait to see!'

'They should follow the snake, instead of catching it. It may lead them to a treasure. All snakes have treasures to guard.'

This seemed to confirm what Ayah had been telling me, and I resolved that I would follow the next snake that I met.

'Don't you like the rose, then?' I asked.

'Did you steal it?'

'Yes.'

'Good. Flowers should always be stolen. They're more fragrant then.'

Because of a man called Hitler war had been declared in Europe and Britain was fighting Germany.

In my comic papers, the Germans were usually shown as blundering idiots; so I didn't see how Britain could possibly lose the war, nor why it should concern India, nor why it should be necessary for my father to join up. But I remember him showing me a newspaper headline which said:

BOMBS FALL ON BUCKINGHAM PALACE—
KING AND QUEEN SAFE

I expect that had something to do with it.

He went to Delhi for an interview with the RAF and I was left in Ayah's charge.

It was a week I remember well, because it was the first time I had been left on my own. That first night I was afraid—afraid of the dark, afraid of the emptiness of the house, afraid of the howling of the jackals outside. The loud ticking of the clock was the only reassuring sound: clocks really made themselves heard in those days! I tried concentrating on the ticking, shutting out other sounds and the menace of the dark, but it wouldn't work. I thought I heard a faint hissing near the bed, and sat up, bathed in perspiration, certain that a snake was in the room. I shouted for Ayah and she came running, switching on all the lights.

'A snake!' I cried. 'There's a snake in the room!'

'Where, baba?'

'I don't know where, but I *heard* it.'

Ayah looked under the bed, and behind the chairs and tables, but there was no snake to be found. She persuaded me that I must have heard the breeze whispering in the mosquito curtains.

But I didn't want to be left alone.

'I'm coming to you,' I said and followed her into her small room near the kitchen.

Ayah slept on a low string cot. The mattress was thin, the blanket worn and patched up; but Ayah's warm and solid body made up for the discomfort of the bed. I snuggled up to her and was soon asleep.

I had almost forgotten the rani in the old palace and was about to pay her a visit when, to my surprise, I found her in the garden. I had risen early that morning, and had gone running barefoot over the dew-drenched grass. No one was about, but

I startled a flock of parrots and the birds rose screeching from a banyan tree and wheeled away to some other corner of the palace grounds. I was just in time to see a mongoose scurrying across the grass with an egg in its mouth. The mongoose must have been raiding the poultry farm at the palace.

I was trying to locate the mongoose's hideout, and was on all fours in a jungle of tall cosmos plants when I heard the rustle of clothes, and turned to find the rani staring at me.

She didn't ask me what I was doing there, but simply said: 'I don't think he could have gone in there.'

'But I saw him go this way,' I said.

'Nonsense! He doesn't live in this part of the garden. He lives in the roots of the banyan tree.'

'But that's where the snake lives,' I said.

'You mean the snake who was a prince. Well, that's whom I'm looking for!'

'A snake who was a prince!' I gaped at the rani.

She made a gesture of impatience with her butterfly hands, and said, 'Tut, you're only a child, you can't understand. The prince lives in the roots of the banyan tree, but he comes out early every morning. Have you seen him?'

'No. But I saw a mongoose.'

The rani became frightened. 'Oh dear, is there a mongoose in the garden? He might kill the prince!'

'How can a mongoose kill a prince?' I asked.

'You don't understand, Master Bond. Princes, when they die, are born again as snakes.'

'*All* princes?'

'No, only those who die before they can marry.'

'Did your prince die before he could marry you?'

'Yes. And he returned to this garden in the form of a beautiful snake.'

'Well,' I said, 'I hope it wasn't the snake the water carrier killed last week.'

'He killed a snake!' The rani looked horrified. She was quivering all over. 'It might have been the prince!'

'It was a brown snake,' I said.

'Oh, then it wasn't him.' She looked very relieved. 'Brown snakes are only ministers and people like that. It has to be a green snake to be a prince.'

'I haven't seen any green snakes here.'

'There's one living in the roots of the banyan tree. You won't kill it, will you?'

'Not if it's really a prince.'

'And you won't let others kill it?'

'I'll tell Ayah.'

'Good. You're on my side. But be careful of the gardener. Keep him away from the banyan tree. He's always killing snakes. I don't trust him at all.'

She came nearer and, leaning forward a little, looked into my eyes.

'Blue eyes—I trust them. But don't trust green eyes. And yellow eyes are evil.'

'I've never seen yellow eyes.'

'That's because you're pure,' she said and turned away and hurried across the lawn as though she had just remembered a very urgent appointment.

The sun was up, slanting through the branches of the banyan tree, and Ayah's voice could be heard calling me for breakfast.

'Dukhi,' I said, when I found him in the garden later that day, 'don't kill the snake in the banyan tree.'

'A snake in the banyan tree!' he exclaimed, seizing his hose.

'No, no!' I said. 'I haven't seen it. But the rani says there's one. She says it was a prince in its former life, and that we shouldn't kill it.'

'Oh,' said Dukhi, smiling to himself. 'The rani says so. All right, you tell her we won't kill it.'

'Is it true that she was in love with a prince but that he died before she could marry him?'

'Something like that,' said Dukhi. 'It was a long time ago—before I came here.'

'My father says it wasn't a prince, but a commoner. Are you a commoner, Dukhi?'

'A commoner? What's that, Chota Sahib?'

'I'm not sure. Someone very poor, I suppose.'

'Then I must be a commoner,' said Dukhi.

'Were you in love with the rani?' I asked.

Dukhi was so startled that he dropped his hose and lost his balance; the first time I'd seen him lose his poise while squatting on his haunches.

'Don't say such things, Chota Sahib!'

'Why not?'

'You'll get me into trouble.'

'Then it must be true.'

Dukhi threw up his hands in mock despair and started collecting his implements.

'It's true, it's true!' I cried, dancing round him, and then I ran indoors to Ayah and said, 'Ayah, Dukhi was in love with the rani!'

Ayah gave a shriek of laughter, then looked very serious and put her finger against my lips.

'Don't say such things,' she said. 'Dukhi is of a very low caste. People won't like it if they hear what you say. And besides, the rani told you her prince died and turned into a snake. Well, Dukhi hasn't become a snake as yet, has he?'

True, Dukhi didn't look as though he could be anything but a gardener; but I wasn't satisfied with his denials or with Ayah's attempts to still my tongue. Hadn't Dukhi sent the rani a nosegay?

When my father came home, he looked quite pleased with himself.

'What have you brought for me?' was the first question I asked.

He had brought me some new books, a dartboard and a train set; and in my excitement over examining these gifts, I forgot to ask about the result of his trip.

It was during tiffin that he told me what had happened—and what was going to happen.

'We'll be going away soon,' he said. 'I've joined the Royal Air Force. I'll have to work in Delhi.'

'Oh! Will you be in the war, Dad? Will you fly a plane?'

'No, I'm too old to be flying planes. I'll be forty years old in July. The RAF will be giving me what they call intelligence work—decoding secret messages and things like that and I don't suppose I'll be able to tell you much about it.'

This didn't sound as exciting as flying planes, but it sounded important and rather mysterious.

'Well, I hope it's interesting,' I said. 'Is Delhi a good place to live in?'

'I'm not sure. It will be very hot by the middle of April. And you won't be able to stay with me, Ruskin—not at first, anyway, not until I can get married quarters and then, only if your mother returns... Meanwhile, you'll stay with your grandmother in Dehra.' He must have seen the disappointment in my face, because he quickly added: 'Of course, I'll come to see you often. Dehra isn't far from Delhi—only a night's train journey.'

But I was dismayed. It wasn't that I didn't want to stay with my grandmother, but I had grown so used to sharing my father's life and even watching him at work, that the thought of being separated from him was unbearable.

'Not as bad as going to boarding school,' he said. 'And that's the only alternative.'

'Not boarding school,' I said quickly, 'I'll run away from boarding school.'

'Well, you won't want to run away from your grandmother. She's very fond of you. And if you come with me to Delhi, you'll be alone all day in a stuffy little hut while I'm away at work. Sometimes I may have to go on tour—then what happens?'

'I don't mind being on my own.' And this was true. I had already grown accustomed to having my own room and my own trunk and my own bookshelf and I felt as though I was about to lose these things.

'Will Ayah come too?' I asked.

My father looked thoughtful. 'Would you like that?'

'Ayah must come,' I said firmly. 'Otherwise I'll run away.'

'I'll have to ask her,' said my father.

Ayah, it turned out, was quite ready to come with us. In fact, she was indignant that Father should have considered leaving her behind. She had brought me up since my mother went away, and she wasn't going to hand over charge to any upstart aunt or governess. She was pleased and excited at the prospect of the move, and this helped to raise my spirits.

'What is Dehra like?' I asked my father.

'It's a green place,' he said. 'It lies in a valley in the foothills of the Himalayas and it's surrounded by forests. There are lots of trees in Dehra.'

'Does Grandmother's house have trees?'

'Yes. There's a big jackfruit tree in the garden. Your grandmother planted it when I was a boy. And there's an old banyan tree, which is good to climb. And there are fruit trees, litchis, mangoes, papayas.'

'Are there any books?'

'Grandmother's books won't interest you. But I'll be bringing you books from Delhi whenever I come to see you.'

I was beginning to look forward to the move. Changing houses had always been fun. Changing towns ought to be fun, too.

A few days before we left, I went to say goodbye to the rani.

'I'm going away,' I said.

'How lovely!' said the rani. 'I wish I could go away!'

'Why don't you?'

'They won't let me. They're afraid to let me out of the palace.'

'What are they afraid of, Your Highness?'

'That I might run away. Run away, far, far away, to the land where the leopards are learning to pray.'

Gosh, I thought, she's really quite crazy… But then she was silent, and started smoking a small hookah.

She drew on the hookah, looked at me, and asked, 'Where is your mother?'

'I haven't one.'

'Everyone has a mother. Did yours die?'

'No. She went away.'

She drew on her hookah again and then said, very sweetly, 'Don't go away…'

'I must,' I said. 'It's because of the war.'

'What war? Is there a war on? You see, no one tells me anything.'

'It's between us and Hitler,' I said.

'And who is Hitler?'

'He's a German.'

'I knew a German once, Dr Schreinherr, he had beautiful hands.'

'Was he an artist?'

'He was a dentist.'

The rani got up from her couch and accompanied me out on to the balcony. When we looked down at the garden, we could see Dukhi weeding a flower bed. Both of us gazed down at him in silence, and I wondered what the rani would say if I asked her if she had ever been in love with the palace gardener. Ayah had told me it would be an insulting question, so I held my peace. But as I walked slowly down the spiral staircase, the rani's voice came after me.

'Thank him,' she said. 'Thank him for the beautiful rose.'

UNTOUCHABLE

The sweeper boy splashed water over the khus matting that hung in the doorway and for a while the air was cooled.

I sat on the edge of my bed, staring out of the open window, brooding upon the dusty road shimmering in the noonday heat. A car passed and the dust rose in billowing clouds.

Across the road lived the people who were supposed to look after me while my father lay in hospital with malaria. I was supposed to stay with them, sleep with them. But except for meals, I kept away. I did not like them and they did not like me.

For a week, longer probably, I was going to live alone in the red-brick bungalow on the outskirts of the town, on the fringe of the jungle. At night the sweeper boy would keep guard, sleeping in the kitchen. Apart from him, I had no company; only the neighbours' children, and I did not like them and they did not like me.

Their mother said, 'Don't play with the sweeper boy, he is unclean. Don't touch him. Remember, he is a servant. You must come and play with my boys.'

Well, I did not intend playing with the sweeper boy; but neither did I intend playing with her children. I was going to sit on my bed all week and wait for my father to come home.

Sweeper boy...all day he pattered up and down between the house and the water tank, with the bucket clanging against his knees.

Back and forth, with a wide, friendly smile.

I frowned at him.

He was about my age, ten. He had short-cropped hair, very white teeth, and muddy feet, hands and face. All he wore was an old pair of khaki shorts; the rest of his body was bare, burnt a deep brown.

At every trip to the water tank he bathed, and returned dripping and glistening from head to toe.

I dripped with sweat.

It was supposedly below my station to bathe at the tank, where the gardener, water-carrier, cooks, ayahs, sweepers and their children all collected. I was the son of a 'sahib' and convention ruled that I did not play with servant children.

But I was just as determined not to play with the other sahibs' children, for I did not like them and they did not like me.

I watched the flies buzzing against the windowpane, the lizards scuttling across the rafters, the wind scattering petals of scorched, long-dead flowers.

The sweeper boy smiled and saluted in play. I avoided his eyes and said, 'Go away.'

He went into the kitchen.

I rose and crossed the room, and lifted my sun helmet off the hatstand.

A centipede ran down the wall, across the floor.

I screamed and jumped on the bed, shouting for help.

The sweeper boy darted in. He saw me on the bed, the centipede on the floor; and picking a large book off the shelf, slammed it down on the repulsive insect.

I remained standing on my bed, trembling with fear and revulsion.

He laughed at me, showing his teeth, and I blushed and said, 'Get out!'

I would not, could not, touch or approach the hat or hatstand. I sat on the bed and longed for my father to come home.

A mosquito passed close by me and sang in my ear. Half-heartedly, I clutched at it and missed; and it disappeared behind the dressing table.

That mosquito, I reasoned, gave the malaria to my father. And now it was trying to give it to me!

The next-door lady walked through the compound and smiled thinly from outside the window. I glared back at her.

The sweeper boy passed with the bucket and grinned. I turned away.

In bed at night, with the lights on, I tried reading. But even books could not quell my anxiety.

The sweeper boy moved about the house, bolting doors, fastening windows. He asked me if I had any orders.

I shook my head.

He skipped across to the electric switch, turned off the light, and slipped into his quarters. Outside, inside, all was dark; only one shaft of light squeezed in through a crack in the sweeper boy's door, and then that too went out.

I began to wish I had stayed with the neighbours. The darkness worried me—silent and close—silent, as if in suspense.

Once a bat flew flat against the window, falling to the ground outside; once an owl hooted. Sometimes a dog barked. And I tautened as a jackal howled hideously in the jungle behind the bungalow. But nothing could break the overall stillness, the night's silence…

Only a dry puff of wind…

It rustled in the trees, and put me in mind of a snake slithering over dry leaves and twigs. I remembered a tale I had been told not long ago, of a sleeping boy who had been bitten by a cobra.

I would not, could not, sleep. I longed for my father...

The shutters rattled, the doors creaked. It was a night for ghosts.

Ghosts!

God, why did I have to think of them?

My God! There, standing by the bathroom door...

My father! My father dead from the malaria and come to see me!

I threw myself at the switch. The room lit up. I sank down on the bed in complete exhaustion, the sweat soaking my nightclothes.

It was not my father I had seen. It was his dressing gown hanging on the bathroom door. It had not been taken with him to the hospital.

I turned off the light.

The hush outside seemed deeper, nearer. I remembered the centipede, the bat, thought of the cobra and the sleeping boy; pulled the sheet tight over my head. If I could see nothing, well then, nothing could see me.

A thunderclap shattered the brooding stillness.

A streak of lightning forked across the sky, so close that even through the sheet I saw a tree and the opposite house silhouetted against the flashing canvas of gold.

I dived deeper beneath the bedclothes, gathered the pillow about my ears.

But at the next thunderclap, louder this time, louder than I had ever heard, I leapt from my bed. I could not stand it. I fled, blundering into the sweeper boy's room.

The boy sat on the bare floor.

'What is happening?' he asked.

The lightning flashed, and his teeth and eyes flashed with it. Then he was a blur in the darkness.

'I am afraid,' I said.

I moved towards him and my hand touched a cold shoulder.

'Stay here,' he said. 'I too am afraid.'

I sat down, my back against the wall; beside the untouchable, the outcaste... And the thunder and lightning ceased, and the rain came down, swishing and drumming on the corrugated roof.

'The rainy season has started,' observed the sweeper boy, turning to me. His smile played with the darkness, and then he laughed. And I laughed too, but feebly.

But I was happy and safe. The scent of the wet earth blew in through the skylight and the rain fell harder.

BHABIJI'S HOUSE

(My neighbours in Rajouri Garden back in the 1960s were the Kamal family. This entry from my journal, which I wrote on one of my later visits, describes a typical day in that household.)

At first light there is a tremendous burst of birdsong from the guava tree in the little garden. Over a hundred sparrows wake up all at once and give tongue to whatever it is that sparrows have to say to each other at five o'clock on a foggy winter's morning in Delhi.

In the small house, people sleep on; that is, everyone except Bhabiji—Granny—the head of the lively Punjabi middle-class family with whom I nearly always stay when I am in Delhi.

She coughs, stirs, groans, grumbles and gets out of bed. The fire has to be lit, and food prepared for two of her sons to take to work. There is a daughter-in-law, Shobha, to help her; but the girl is not very efficient at getting up in the morning. Actually, it is this way: Bhabiji wants to show up her daughter-in-law; so, no matter how hard Shobha tries to be up first, Bhabiji forestalls her. The old lady does not sleep well, anyway; her eyes are open long before the first sparrow chirps, and as soon as she sees her daughter-in-law stirring, she scrambles out of bed and hurries to the kitchen. This gives her the opportunity to say: 'What good is a daughter-in-law when I have to get up to prepare her husband's food?'

The truth is that Bhabiji does not like anyone else preparing her sons' food. She looks no older than when I first saw her ten years ago. She still has complete control over a large family and, with tremendous confidence and enthusiasm, presides over the lives of three sons, a daughter, two daughters-in-law and fourteen grandchildren. This is a joint family (there are not many left in a big city like Delhi), in which the sons and their families all live together as one unit under their mother's benevolent (and sometimes slightly malevolent) autocracy. Even when her husband was alive, Bhabiji dominated the household.

The eldest son, Shiv, has a separate kitchen, but his wife and children participate in all the family celebrations and quarrels. It is a small miracle how everyone (including myself when I visit) manages to fit into the house; and a stranger might be forgiven for wondering where everyone sleeps, for no beds are visible during the day. That is because the beds—light wooden frames with rough string across—are brought in only at night, and are taken out first thing in the morning and kept in the garden shed.

As Bhabiji lights the kitchen fire, the household begins to stir, and Shobha joins her mother-in-law in the kitchen. As a guest, I am privileged and may get up last. But my bed soon becomes an island battered by waves of scurrying, shouting children—eager to bathe, dress, eat and find their school books. Before I can get up, someone brings me a tumbler of hot sweet tea. It is a brass tumbler and burns my fingers; I have yet to learn how to hold one properly. Punjabis like their tea with lots of milk and sugar—so much so that I often wonder why they bother to add any tea.

Ten years ago, 'bed tea' was unheard of in Bhabiji's house. Then, the first time I came to stay, Kamal, the youngest son, told Bhabiji: 'My friend is Angrez. He must have tea in bed.'

He forgot to mention that I usually took my morning cup at seven; they gave it to me at five. I gulped it down and went to sleep again. Then, slowly, others in the household began indulging in morning cups of tea. Now everyone, including the older children, has 'bed tea'. They bless my English forebears for instituting the custom; I bless the Punjabis for perpetuating it.

Breakfast is by rota, in the kitchen. It is a tiny room and accommodates only four adults at a time. The children have eaten first; but the smallest children, Shobha's toddlers, keep coming in and climbing over us. Says Bhabiji of the youngest and most mischievous: 'He lives only because God keeps a special eye on him.'

Kamal, his elder brother Arun and I sit cross-legged and barefooted on the floor while Bhabiji serves us hot parathas stuffed with potatoes and onions, along with omelettes, an excellent dish. Arun then goes to work on his scooter, while Kamal catches a bus for the city, where he attends an art college. After they have gone, Bhabiji and Shobha have their breakfast.

By nine o'clock everyone who is still in the house is busy doing something. Shobha is washing clothes. Bhabiji has settled down on a cot with a huge pile of spinach, which she methodically cleans and chops up. Madhu, her fourteen-year-old granddaughter, who attends school only in the afternoons, is washing down the sitting-room floor. Madhu's mother is a teacher in a primary school in Delhi, and earns a pittance of ₹150 a month. Her husband went to England ten years ago, and never returned; he does not send any money home.

Madhu is made attractive by the gravity of her countenance. She is always thoughtful, reflective; seldom speaks, smiles rarely (but looks very pretty when she does). I wonder what she thinks about as she scrubs floors, prepares meals with Bhabiji, washes dishes and even finds a few hard-pressed moments for her school work. She is the Cinderella of the house. Not that she has to put up with anything like a cruel stepmother. Madhu is Bhabiji's favourite. She has made herself so useful that she is above all reproach. Apart from that, there is a certain measure of aloofness about her—she does not get involved in domestic squabbles—and this is foreign to a household in which everyone has something to say for himself or herself. Her two young brothers are constantly being reprimanded; but no one says anything to Madhu. Only yesterday morning, when clothes were being washed and Madhu was scrubbing the floor, the following dialogue took place.

Madhu's mother (picking up a school book left in the courtyard): 'Where's that boy Popat? See how careless he is with his books! Popat! He's run off. Just wait till he gets back. I'll give him a good beating.'

Vinod's mother: 'It's not Popat's book. It's Vinod's. Where's Vinod?'

Vinod (grumpily): 'It's Madhu's book.'

Silence for a minute or two. Madhu continues scrubbing the floor; she does not bother to look up. Vinod picks up the book and takes it indoors. The women return to their chores.

Manju, daughter of Shiv and sister of Vinod, is averse to housework and, as a result, is always being scolded—by her parents, grandmother, uncles and aunts.

Now, she is engaged in the unwelcome chore of sweeping the front yard. She does this with a sulky look, ignoring my cheerful remarks. I have been sitting under the guava tree, but Manju soon sweeps me away from this spot. She creates a drifting cloud of dust, and seems satisfied only when the dust settles on the clothes that have just been hung up to dry. Manju is a sensuous creature and, like most sensuous people, is lazy by nature. She does not like sweeping because the boy next door can see her at it, and she wants to appear before him in a more glamorous light. Her first action every morning is to turn to the cinema advertisements in the newspaper. Bombay's movie moguls cater for girls like Manju, who long to be tragic heroines. Life is so very dull for middle-class teenagers in Delhi that it is only natural that they should lean so heavily on escapist entertainment. Every residential area has a cinema. But there is not a single bookshop in this particular suburb, although it has a population of over 20,000 literate people. Few children read books; but they are adept at swotting up examination 'guides'; and students of, say, Hardy or Dickens read the guides and not the novels.

Bhabiji is now grinding onions and chillies in a mortar. Her eyes are watering but she is in a good mood. Shobha sits quietly in the kitchen. A little while ago she was complaining to me of a backache. I am the only one who lends a sympathetic ear to complaints of aches and pains. But since last night, my sympathies have been under severe strain. When I got into bed at about ten o'clock, I found the sheets wet. Apparently Shobha had put her baby to sleep in my bed during the afternoon.

While the housework is still in progress, cousin Kishore arrives. He is an itinerant musician who makes a living by arranging performances at marriages. He visits Bhabiji's house frequently and at odd hours, often a little tipsy, always brimming over with goodwill and grandiose plans for the future. It was once his ambition to be a film producer, and some years back he lost a lot of Bhabiji's money in producing a film that was never completed. He still talks of finishing it.

'Brother,' he says, taking me into his confidence for the hundredth time, 'do you know anyone who has a movie camera?'

'No,' I say, knowing only too well how these admissions can lead me into a morass of complicated manoeuvres. But Kishore is not easily put off, especially when he has been fortified with country liquor.

'But you *knew* someone with a movie camera?' he asks.

'That was long ago.'

'How long ago?' (I have got him going now.)

'About five years back.'

'Only five years? Find him, find him!'

'It's no use. He doesn't have the movie camera any more. He sold it.'

'Sold it!' Kishore looks at me as though I have done him an injury. 'But why didn't you buy it? All we need is a movie camera, and our fortune is made. I will produce the film, I will direct it, I will write the music. Two in one, Charlie Chaplin and Raj Kapoor. Why didn't you buy the camera?'

'Because I didn't have the money.'

'But we could have borrowed the money.'

'If you are in a position to borrow money, you can go out and buy another movie camera.'

'We could have borrowed the camera. Do you know anyone else who has one?'

'Not a soul.' I am firm this time; I will not be led into another maze.

'Very sad, very sad,' mutters Kishore. And with a dejected, hangdog expression designed to make me feel that I am responsible for all his failures, he moves off.

Bhabiji had expressed some annoyance at his arrival, but he softens her up by leaving behind an invitation to a marriage party this evening. No one in the house knows the bride's or bridegroom's family, but that does not matter; knowing one of the musicians is just as good. Almost everyone will go.

While Bhabiji, Shobha and Madhu are preparing lunch, Bhabiji engages in one of her favourite subjects of conversation, Kamal's marriage, which she hopes she will be able to arrange in the near future. She freely acknowledges that she made grave blunders in selecting wives for her other sons—this is meant to be heard by Shobha—and promises not to repeat her mistakes. According to Bhabiji, Kamal's bride should be both educated and domesticated; and of course, she must be fair.

'What if he likes a dark girl?' I ask teasingly.

Bhabiji looks horrified. 'He cannot marry a dark girl,' she declares.

'But dark girls are beautiful,' I tell her.

'Impossible!'

'Do you want him to marry a European girl?'

'No foreigners! I know them, they'll take my son away. He shall have a good Punjabi girl, with a complexion the colour of wheat.'

Noon. The shadows shift and cross the road. I sit beneath the guava tree and watch the women at work. They will not let me do anything, but they like talking to me and they love to hear my broken Punjabi. Sparrows flit about at their feet, snapping up the grain that runs away from their busy fingers. A crow looks speculatively at the empty kitchen, sidles towards the open door; but Bhabiji has only to glance up and the experienced crow flies away. He knows he will not be able to make off with anything from this house.

One by one the children come home, demanding food. Now it is Madhu's turn to go to school. Her younger brother Popat, an intelligent but undersized boy of thirteen, appears in the doorway and asks for lunch.

'Be off!' says Bhabiji. 'It isn't ready yet.'

Actually the food is ready and only the chapattis remain to be made. Shobha will attend to them. Bhabiji lies down on her cot in the sun, complaining of a pain in her back and ringing noises in her ears.

'I'll press your back,' says Popat. He has been out of

Bhabiji's favour lately, and is looking for an opportunity to be rehabilitated.

Barefooted, he stands on Bhabiji's back and treads her weary flesh and bones with a gentle walking-in-one-spot movement. Bhabiji grunts with relief. Every day she has new pains in new places. Her age, and the daily business of feeding the family and running everyone's affairs, are beginning to tell on her. But she would sooner die than give up her position of dominance in the house. Her working sons still hand over their pay to her, and she dispenses the money as she sees fit.

The pummelling she gets from Popat puts her in a better mood, and she holds forth on another favourite subject, the respective merits of various dowries. Shiv's wife (according to Bhabiji) brought nothing with her but a string cot; Kishore's wife brought only a sharp and clever tongue; Shobha brought a wonderful steel cupboard, fully expecting that it would do all the housework for her.

This last observation upsets Shobha, and a little later I find her under the guava tree, weeping profusely. I give her the comforting words she obviously expects; but it is her husband Arun who will have to bear the brunt of her outraged feelings when he comes home this evening. He is rather nervous of his wife. Last night he wanted to eat out, at a restaurant, but did not want to be accused of wasting money; so he stuffed fifteen rupees into my pocket and asked me to invite both him and Shobha to dinner, which I did.

We had a good dinner. Such unexpected hospitality on my part has further improved my standing with Shobha. Now, in spite of other chores, she sees that I get cups of tea and coffee at odd hours of the day.

Bhabiji knows Arun is soft with his wife, and taunts him about it. She was saying this morning that whenever there is any work to be done, Shobha retires to bed with a headache (partly true). She says even Manju does more housework (not true). Bhabiji has certain talents as an actress, and does a good take-off of Shobha sulking and grumbling at having too much to do.

While Bhabiji talks, Popat sneaks off and goes for a ride on the bicycle. It is a very old bicycle and is constantly undergoing repairs. 'The soul has gone out of it,' says Vinod philosophically and makes his way on to the roof, where he keeps a store of pornographic literature. Up there, he cannot be seen and cannot be remembered, and so avoids being sent out on errands.

One of the boys is bathing at the hand-pump. Manju, who should have gone to school with Madhu, is stretched out on a cot, complaining of fever. But she will be up in time to attend the marriage party…

Towards evening, as the birds return to roost in the guava tree, their chatter is challenged by the tumult of people in the house, getting ready for the marriage party.

Manju presses her tight pyjamas but neglects to darn them. She wears a loose-fitting, diaphanous shirt. She keeps flitting in and out of the front room so that I can admire the way she glitters. Shobha has used too much powder and lipstick in an effort to look like the femme fatale which she indubitably is not. Shiv's more conservative wife floats around in loose, old-fashioned pyjamas. Bhabiji is sober and austere in a white sari. Madhu looks neat. The men wear their suits.

Popat is holding up a mirror for his Uncle Kishore, who is combing his long hair. (Kishore kept his hair long, like a court musician at the time of Akbar, before the hippies had been heard of.) He is nodding benevolently, having fortified himself from a bottle labelled 'Som Ras' ('Nectar of the Gods'), obtained cheaply from an illicit still.

Kishore: 'Don't shake the mirror, boy!'

Popat: 'Uncle, it's your head that's shaking.'

Shobha is happy. She loves going out, especially to marriages, and she always takes her two small boys with her, although they invariably spoil the carpets.

Only Kamal, Popat and I remain behind. I have had more than my share of marriage parties.

The house is strangely quiet. It does not seem so small now, with only three people left in it. The kitchen has been locked (Bhabiji will not leave it open while Popat is still in the house), so we visit the dhaba, the wayside restaurant near the main road, and this time I pay the bill with my own money. We have kababs and chicken curry.

Yesterday, Kamal and I took our lunch on the grass of the Buddha Jayanti Gardens (Buddha's Birthday Gardens). There was no college for Kamal, as the majority of Delhi's students had hijacked a number of corporation buses and headed for the Pakistan High Commission, with every intention of levelling it to the ground if possible, as a protest against the hijacking of an Indian plane from Srinagar to Lahore. The students were met by the Delhi police in full strength, and a pitched battle took place, in which stones from the students and tear gas shells from the police were the favoured missiles. There were two shells fired every minute, according to a newspaper report. And this went on all day. A number of students and policemen were injured, but by some miracle, no one was killed. The police held their ground, and the Pakistan High Commission remained inviolate. But the Australian High Commission, situated to the rear of the student brigade, received most of the tear gas shells, and had to close down for the day.

Kamal and I attended the siege for about an hour, before retiring to the Gardens with our ham sandwiches. A couple of friendly squirrels came up to investigate, and were soon taking bread from our hands. We could hear the chanting of the students in the distance. I lay back on the grass and opened my copy of *Barchester Towers*. Whenever life in Delhi, or in Bhabiji's house (or anywhere, for that matter), becomes too tumultuous, I turn to Trollope. Nothing could be further removed from the turmoil of our times than an English cathedral town in the nineteenth century. But I think Jane Austen would have appreciated life in Bhabiji's house.

By ten o'clock, everyone is back from the marriage. (They had gone for the feast, and not for the ceremonies, which continue into the early hours of the morning.) Shobha is full of praise for the bridegroom's good looks and fair complexion. She describes him as being 'gora-chitta'—very white! She does not have a high opinion of the bride.

Shiv, in a happy and reflective mood, extols the qualities of his own wife, referring to her as The Barrel. He tells us how, shortly after their marriage, she had threatened to throw a brick at the next-door girl. This little incident remains fresh in Shiv's mind, after eighteen years of marriage.

He says: 'When the neighbours came and complained, I told them, "It is quite possible that my wife will throw a brick at your daughter. She is in the habit of throwing bricks." The neighbours held their peace.'

I think Shiv is rather proud of his wife's militancy when it comes to taking on neighbours; recently she vanquished the woman next door (a formidable Sikh lady) after a verbal battle that lasted three hours. But in arguments or quarrels with Bhabiji, Shiv's wife always loses, because Shiv takes his mother's side. Arun, on the other hand, is afraid of both wife and mother, and simply makes himself scarce when a quarrel develops. Or he tells his mother she is right, and then, to placate Shobha, takes her to the pictures.

Kishore turns up just as everyone is about to go to bed. Bhabiji is annoyed at first, because he has been drinking too much; but when he produces a bunch of cinema tickets, she is mollified and asks him to stay the night. Not even Bhabiji likes missing a new picture.

Kishore is urging me to write his life story.

'Your life would make a most interesting story,' I tell him. 'But it will be interesting only if I put in everything—your successes *and* your failures.'

'No, no, only successes,' exhorts Kishore. 'I want you to describe me as a popular music director.'

'But you have yet to become popular.'

'I will be popular if you write about me.'

Fortunately, we are interrupted by the cots being brought in. Then Bhabiji and Shiv go into a huddle, discussing plans for building an extra room. After all, Kamal may be married soon.

One by one, the children get under their quilts. Popat starts massaging Bhabiji's back. She gives him her favourite blessing: 'God protect you and give you lots of children.' If God listens to all Bhabiji's prayers and blessings, there will never be a fall in the population.

The lights are off and Bhabiji settles down for the night. She is almost asleep when a small voice pipes up: 'Bhabiji, tell us a story.'

At first Bhabiji pretends not to hear; then, when the request is repeated, she says: 'You'll keep Aunty Shobha awake, and then she'll have an excuse for getting up late in the morning.' But the children know Bhabiji's one great weakness, and they renew their demand.

'Your grandmother is tired,' says Arun. 'Let her sleep.'

But Bhabiji's eyes are open. Her mind is going back over the crowded years, and she remembers something very interesting that happened when her younger brother's wife's sister married the eldest son of her third cousin...

Before long, the children are asleep, and I am wondering if I will ever sleep, for Bhabiji's voice drones on, into the darker reaches of the night.

FLOWERS ON THE GANGA

Flowers floating down the river: yellow and scarlet cannas, roses, jasmine, hibiscus. They are placed in boats made of broad leaves; then consigned to the waters with a prayer. The strong current carries them swiftly downstream, and they bob about on the water for fifty, sometimes a hundred yards, before being submerged in the river. Do the prayers sink too, or do they reach the hearts of the many gods who have favoured Haridwar—'Door of Hari or Vishnu'—these several hundred years?

The river issues through a gorge in the mountains with a low booming sound. It does not break its banks until it levels out over the flat plains of Uttar Pradesh and Bihar. It is fast and muddy; but this does not deter thousands from descending the steps of the bathing ghats and plunging into the cold, snow-fed waters, for the Ganga washes away all sin.

Says the Mahabharata: 'To repeat her name brings purity, to see her secures prosperity, to bathe in or drink her waters saves seven generations of our race... There is no place of pilgrimage like the Ganga, no god like Vishnu...'

Almost every child knows the story of how the Ganga descended from heaven. For 1,000 years, King Sagara's great-grandson stood with his hands upraised, praying for water to enable him to make the funeral oblations for the ashes of his 60,000 grand-uncles. Almost all the gods were involved in the affair. Finally, when the waters of the Ganga were released from heaven and the river reached the earth, the prince mounted his chariot and drove towards the spot where the ashes of his kinsmen lay. Wherever he went, the Ganga meekly followed. Gods, nymphs, demons, giants, sages and great snakes, all joined in the procession, and as the river followed in the footsteps of the prince, the whole multitude of created beings bathed in her sacred waters and washed away their sins.

◆

The multitude that followed the prince could be the same multitude that throngs the riverfront today. I see no one who is not delighted at the prospect of entering the water. '*Ganga-Mai ki jai*!' The cry goes up mostly from the older people who have come here, many for the last time, to make their peace with the gods. Only their ashes will make the trip again.

It is a big crowd, although this is just an ordinary day of the week and not an occasion of special religious significance. Every day is a good day for bathing in the Ganga. But at the time of major festivals, such as Baisakhi, elaborate arrangements have to be made, including special trains and police reinforcements, to take care of the great influx of pilgrims. The number of pilgrims at the Baisakhi festival usually exceeds one lakh. During the Kumbh Mela, held every twelve years, there may be as many as five lakh present on the great bathing-day. This is ten times the normal population of Haridwar. And when one realizes that the town is bounded by the steep Siwalik Hills on one side and the river on the other, and has one main street leading to the riverfront, it is not surprising that in the past, large numbers of people were crushed to death in stampedes at the narrow entrance to the ghats.

Fortunately the main street is a broad and pleasant thoroughfare. Although Haridwar is ancient (the Chinese traveller, Hsuen Tsang, records a visit made in the seventh century), little remains of earlier settlements. There are only two or three old temples. But the present buildings—tall, balconied structures put up in the 1920s and 1930s have a certain old-world charm. Even new houses follow the same pattern. This isn't conscious planning; it is simply that Haridwar is a conservative town and clings to its traditions.

Most of the buildings along the road are *dharamshalas*. The road is shaded by tall old peepul and banyan trees. In some places the trees reach right across the street to touch the roofs of the three-storey buildings on the other side. At several places, I find small peepul saplings growing out of the walls of buildings. One young peepul has sprung up in the fork of an adult kadam tree and will probably throttle it in time. No one fells the sacred peepul. It is better that walls should crumble or kadam trees wither. At least this guarantees the survival of one species of tree in a world where forests are rapidly disappearing.

Peepuls live for hundreds of years, and Haridwar's oldest trees must have been here before the present town reached maturity. Some will be as old as the eleventh-century Maya-devi temple, which is probably the oldest temple in Haridwar. On a sultry day, there can be no pleasanter spot than the shade of a peepul tree; the leaves are perpetually in motion, even when there is no breeze, and spin around in currents of their own making. It is no wonder that the man who plants a peepul is blessed by generations of Hindus to come.

While I stand beneath one of these giant trees, a devout and elderly man approaches with a watering-can and, circling the tree, waters the soil around the base of the trunk. I move out of the way of his sprinkler watching the ritual in some surprise. It has been raining steadily for some days, and the tree should have no need of water.

'Why are you watering it?' I ask.

'Why does one water anything?' asks the old man. 'So that it may grow and flourish, of course.'

'But it's been raining almost every day.'

'Rain is something else,' he says. 'I am not responsible for the rain; this is water from the Ganga, and I have fetched it myself. That makes a lot of difference.'

I cannot argue. He waters the tree with love; and his love for the tree, as much as rainwater or river water, is what makes it flourish.

Leaving the main street, I enter the bazaar.

The Haridwar Bazaar is a long, narrow, winding street, probably the oldest part of the town, and free of all vehicular traffic. The road is no more than four yards wide. The small shops are spilling over with sweets, pickles, bead-necklaces, sacred texts, ritual designs, festival images and pictures of the gods in vibrant technicolour. There is something in these naive, gaudy prints that acts as a transformer, making the more abstract Hindu philosophies comprehensible to anxious farmer or acquisitive taxi driver.

The bazaar winds and turns back upon itself, and eventually I find myself back at the riverfront, gazing out across the river at the forested foothills. Few of the pilgrims on the bathing-steps can realize that sometimes at night a tiger stands on the opposite bank watching the bright illuminations of the temples, or that elephants listen to the rumbling of the trains bringing pilgrims to Haridwar from all parts of India.

It is evening now, and there are fewer people at the ghats. Most of the bathers are family people—farmers and small shopkeepers with their women, children and aged parents. One does not see many students or young people in Western clothes. Haridwar is old- fashioned and so are most of the people who come here.

◆

Charity, too, is old-fashioned, and Haridwar thrives on charity: donations to the temples and alms to the beggars, mendicants and itinerant ash-smeared sadhus. The beggars do not follow one about as in the larger cities. They are confident of receiving coins from the pilgrims who pass by on the steps to the river. They simply sit there, occasionally calling out, but preferring to listen to the music of small coins dropping into brass begging-bowls.

Close by are the money changers, squatting before baskets which are brimming over with small change. In the rest of the country there is a shortage of small coins, and shopkeepers often decline to provide change; but in Haridwar, you can change any number of notes for small coins. You are going to leave all the coins here anyway, when you distribute them along the riverfront.

As the pilgrims leave the ghats, the joy of having accomplished their mission bursts forth in songs of praise: 'Henceforth no more pain, no more sickness; all will be well in future; Ganga-mai ki jai.

More flowers are being sold; and now the leaf-boats are lit by diyas. The little boats are swept away, sometimes travelling a considerable distance before being upset by submerged rocks or inquisitive fish.

I, too, send an offering downstream, but my boat sails beneath the legs of a late bather, and disappears beneath the pilgrim. My boat is lost; but my rose petals still float on the Ganga.

It has been said that if the Ganga ran dry, all life in India would cease. There is no likelihood of that happening. The Ganga is overgenerous as the annual floods will testify. So long as the

Himalayas stand, this river will flow to the sea and millions will come to immerse their bodies, their sins and their prayers in its sacred waters.

GREAT TREES OF GARHWAL

Living for many years in a cottage at 7,000 ft in the Garhwal Himalayas, I was fortunate to have a big window that opened out on the forest, so that the trees were almost within my reach. Had I jumped, I should have landed quite safely in the arms of an oak or chestnut.

The incline of the hill was such that my first floor window opened on what must, I suppose, have been the second floor of the tree. I never made the jump, but the big langurs—silver grey monkeys with long swishing tails—often leapt from the trees onto the corrugated tin roof and made enough noise to disturb the bats sleeping in the space between the roof and ceiling.

Standing on its own was a walnut tree, and truly this was a tree for all seasons. In winter the branches were bare; but they were smooth and straight and round like the arms of a woman in a painting by Jamini Roy. In the spring, each branch produced a hard, bright spear of new leaf. By midsummer the entire tree was in leaf; and towards the end of the monsoon, the walnuts, encased in their green jackets, had reached maturity.

Then the jackets began to split, revealing the hard brown shell of the walnuts. Inside the shell was the nut itself. Look closely at the nut and you will notice that it is shaped rather like the human brain. No wonder the ancients prescribed walnuts for headaches!

Every year the tree gave me a basket of walnuts. But last

year the walnuts were disappearing one by one, and I was at a loss to know who had been taking them. Could it have been Bijju, the milkman's son? He was an inveterate tree climber. But he was usually to be found on oak trees, gathering fodder for his cows. He told me that his cows liked oak leaves but did not care for walnuts. He admitted that they had relished my dahlias, which they had eaten the previous week, but he denied having fed them walnuts.

It wasn't the woodpecker. He was out there every day, knocking furiously against the bark of the tree, trying to prise an insect out of a narrow crack. He was strictly non-vegetarian and none the worse for it.

One day I found a fat langur sitting in the walnut tree. I watched him for some time to see if he was going to help himself to the nuts, but he was only sunning himself. When he thought I wasn't looking, he came down and ate the geraniums; but he did not take any walnuts.

The walnuts had been disappearing early in the morning while I was still in bed. So one morning I surprised everyone, including myself, by getting up before sunrise. I was just in time to catch the culprit climbing out of the walnut tree.

She was an old woman, who sometimes came to cut grass on the hillside. Her face was as wrinkled as the walnuts she had been helping herself to. In spite of her age, her arms and legs were sturdy. When she saw me, she was as swift as a civet cat in getting out of the tree.

'And how many walnuts did you gather today, Grandmother?' I asked.

'Only two,' she said with a giggle, offering them to me on her open palm. I accepted one of them. Encouraged, she climbed back into the tree and helped herself to the remaining nuts. It was impossible to object. I was taken up in admiration of her agility in the tree. She must have been about sixty, and I was a mere forty-five, but I knew I would never be climbing trees again.

To the victor the spoils!

The horse chestnuts are inedible, even the monkeys throw them away in disgust. Once, on passing beneath a horse chestnut tree, a couple of chestnuts bounched off my head. Looking up, I saw that they had been dropped on me by a couple of mischievous rhesus monkeys.

The tree itself is a friendly one, especially in summer when it is full leaf. The least breath of wind makes the leaves break into conversation, and their rustle is a cheerful sound, unlike the sad notes of pine trees in the wind. The spring flowers look like candelabra, and when the blossoms fall they carpet the hillside with their pale pink petals.

We pass now to my favourite tree, the deodar. In Garhwal and Kumaon it is called Dujar or Devdar; in Jaunsar and parts of Himachal it is known as the Kelu or Kelon. It is also identified with the cedar of Lebanon (the cones are identical), although the deodar's needles are slightly longer and more bluish. Trees, like humans, change with their environment. Several persons familiar with the deodar at Indian hill-stations, when asked to point it out in London's Kew Gardens, indicated the cedar of Lebanon; and when shown a deodar, declared that they had never seen this tree in the Himalayas!

We shall stick to the name deodar, which comes from the Sanskrit *Deva-daru* (divine tree). It is a sacred tree in the Himalayas; not worshipped, not protected in the way that a peepul is in the plains, but sacred in that its timber has always been used in temples, for doors, windows, walls and even roofs. Quite frankly, I would just as soon worship the deodar as worship anything, for in its beauty and majesty it represents Nature in its most noble aspect.

No one who has lived amongst deodars would deny that it is the most godlike of Himalayan trees. It stands erect, dignified; and though in a strong wind it may hum and sigh and moan, it does not bend to the wind. The snow slips softly from its resilient branches. In the spring the new leaves are tender green, while during the monsoon the tiny young cones spread like blossoms in the dark green folds of the branches. The deodar thrives in the rain and enjoys the company of its own kind. Where one deodar grows, there will be others. Isolate a young tree and it will often pine away.

The great deodar forests are found along the upper reaches of the Bhagirathi valley and the Tons in Garhwal; and in Himachal and Kashmir, along the Chenab and the Jhelum, and also the Kishenganga; it is at its best between 7,000 and 9,000 ft. I had expected to find it on the upper reaches of Alaknanda, but could not find a single deodar along the road to Badrinath. That particular valley seems hostile to trees in general, and deodars in particular.

The average girth of the deodar is 15–20 ft, but individual trees often attain a great size. Records show that one great deodar was 250 ft high, 20 ft in girth at the base, and more than five hundred and fifty years old. The timber of these trees, which is unaffected by extremes of climate, was always highly prized for house buildings; and in the villages of Jaunsar Bawar, finely carved doors and windows are a feature of the timbered dwellings. Many of the quaint old bridges over the Jhelum in Kashmir are supported on pillars fashioned from whole deodar trees; some of these bridges are more than five hundred years old.

To return to my own trees, I went among them often, acknowledging their presence with the touch of my hand against their trunks—the walnut's smooth and polished; the pine's patterned and whorled; and oak's rough, gnarled, full of experience. The oak had been there the longest, and the wind had bent his upper branches and twisted a few, so that he looked shaggy and undistinguished. It is a good tree for the privacy of birds, its crooked branches spreading out with no particular effect; and sometimes the tree seems uninhabited until there is a whirring sound, as of a helicopter approaching, and a party of long-tailed blue magpies stream across the forest glade.

After the monsoon, when the dark red berries had ripened on the hawthorn, this pretty tree was visited by green pigeons, the kokla birds of Garhwal, who clambered upside-down among the fruit-laden twigs. And during winter, a white-capped redstart perched on the bare branches of the wild pear tree and whistled cheerfully. He had come down from higher places to winter in the garden.

The pines grow on the next hill—the chir, the Himalayan blue pine, and the long leaved pine—but there is a small blue pine a little way below the cottage, and sometimes I sit beneath it to listen to the wind playing softly in its branches.

Open the window at night and there is usually something to listen to: the mellow whistle of a pigmy owlet, or the cry of a barking deer which has scented the proximity of a panther. Sometimes, if you are lucky, you will see the moon coming up over Nag Tibba and two distant deodars in perfect silhouette.

Some sounds cannot be recognized. They are strange night sounds, the sounds of the trees themselves, stretching their limbs in the dark, shifting a little, flexing their fingers. Great trees of the mountains, they know me well. They know my face in the window; they see me watching them, watching them grow, listening to their secrets, bowing my head before their outstretched arms and seeking their benediction.

TALES OF OLD MUSSOORIE

At one time visitors to Mussoorie frequently found themselves persuaded to climb to the top of a local peak called 'Gun Hill', from which one is able to obtain a view of the greater Himalayas. Today a cable-car takes tourists to the top of the hill, from which, besides the snows, Mussoorie waterworks, too, can be seen, but of a 'gun' there is no sign and they may be pardoned for wondering how the hill acquired its impressive name. We hope to enlighten them on this, and other aspects, of the hill-station's distant though not ancient past.

Before 1919, noon-time was indicated by the firing of a cannon from the top of 'Gun Hill', possibly because cannons were cheaper than clocks in those days. At first the gun faced east; then soon after its installation, a complaint came from the Grey Castle Nursing Home that the gun when fired 'often let loose plaster from the ceiling of the wards, which fell on patients' beds and unnerved them'. It could not be pointed north because it would then have blasted away a house called 'Dilkush'; so it was faced north-east, but that again couldn't be made its permanent position, for the Crystal Bank then complained. Turned to the south, it almost succeeded in fulfilling its legitimate duty, but that was before the gunner forgot to remove the ramrod from the barrel; and on booming noon to the populace, the cannon sent the ramrod clean through the roof of the Savoy hotel.

Public opinion consequently was mounting against the gun, and it was turned around once more to face the Mall. The boom was usually produced by ramming down the barrel a mixture of moist grass and cotton waste, after the powder was in place. Due to an accidental overcharge of powder, one of these cannon-balls landed with some force right in the lap of a lady who was being taken along the Mall in a rickshaw. It was the last straw or, to be exact, the last cannon-ball, for the gun was dismantled soon after the incident.

A peep into the life of the hill-station before the turn of the century is a fascinating exercise; but before giving the reader further anecdotes, we should fill in the background with a brief historical sketch of the hill-station.

In the year 1825, the superintendent of the Doon was a certain Mr Shore, who occasionally found time from his official duties to scramble up the range, then known as 'Mansuri' because of the prevalence of a shrub known in the vernacular as the Mansur plant. He found that the range had a number of 'flats', some of which accommodated the huts of cowherds who grazed their cattle on them during the summer months. The hills were then well forested and game plentiful; so the first construction was a shooting-box built jointly by Mr Shore and Captain Young of the Sirmur Rifles. It has long since disappeared, but is said to have been located on the Camel's Back, facing north. The first home—still recognizable—was 'Mullingar' in Landour, built in 1826 by Captain Young. Landour soon became a convalescent depot for British troops; the old convalescent hospital now forms the nucleus of the offices of the Defence Institute of Work Study. Soon civilians were flocking to Mussoorie, building houses as far apart as 'Cloud End' to the west and 'Dahlia Bank' to the east, separated by some twelve miles. In 1832, Colonel Everest (after whom the mountain is named) as Surveyor-General opened his Survey of India office in 'The Park' and made a road to it.

People came to Mussoorie for health, business and pleasure; and amongst the pleasure-seekers we find the Hon'ble Emily Eden, sister of Lord George Eden, Earl of Auckland, Governor General of India. One of our earliest visitors, she records in her famous diaries that 'in the afternoon we took a beautiful ride up to Landour, but the paths are very narrow on that side, and our courage somehow oozed out, and first we came to a place where they said, "This was where poor Major Blundell and his pony fell over and they were both dashed to atoms," and then there was a board stuck in a tree, "From this spot a private in the Cameroons fell and was killed..." We had to get off our ponies and lead them, and altogether I thought much of poor Major Blundell. It is impossible to imagine more beautiful scenery'.

Though there were no proper roads in Mussoorie in those early days, some of the cliff-edge accidents were undoubtedly caused by the beer that was then so cheap and plentiful in the hill-station.

Mr Bohle, one of the pioneers of brewing in India, started the 'Old Brewery' near Hathipaon in 1830. Two years later he got into trouble for supplying beer to soldiers who were alleged to have presented forged passes. Mr Bohle was called to account by Captain (by now Colonel) Young for distilling spirits without a license, and had to close his concern. Undaunted, he was back in 1834, building 'Bohle's Brewery', and became a popular figure in Mussoorie society. His tomb in the Camel's Back cemetery is still one of the most impressive.

Scandal again erupted in the brewery business in 1876, when everyone suddenly started talking of a much improved brew. It came from Vat 42 in Whymer and Company's 'Crown Brewery'. The beer was retasted until the diminishing level of the barrel revealed the perfectly brewed remains of a human! Someone had fallen into the vat and been drowned, and, all unknown to himself, had given the beer-trade a real fillip. The author of *A Mussoorie Miscellany* (H.C. Williams) informs us that 'meat was thereafter recognized as the missing component and scrupulosuly added till more modern, and less cannibalistic, means were discovered to satiate the froth-blower'.

A bold, bad place was Mussoorie in those days, according to the correspondent of the *Statesman,* who, in his paper of 22 October 1884, wrote 'Ladies and gentlemen, after attending church, proceeded to a drinking shop, a restaurant adjoining the library, and there indulged freely in pegs, not one but many; and at a Fancy Bazaar held this season, a lady stood up on her chair and offered her kisses to gentlemen at Rs 5 each. What would they think of such a state of society at home?'

Fifty years later, a Mussoorie lady auctioned a single kiss for Rs 300. A vivid illustration of the inflationary process throughout history.

But inspite of such goings-on, or perhaps because of them, the inhabitants were conscious of their spiritual needs, and a number of churches were soon dotted about the hill-station, the oldest of them being Christ Church (1836).

When, in March 1905, Her Royal Highness the Princess of Wales (later Queen Mary) visited Mussoorie, she planted a deodar tree outside Christ Church. The plaque commemorating this event can still be seen, now almost embedded in the trunk of the tree.

Some thirty years later, the chaplain of Christ Church was the fair-minded Reverend T.W. Chisolm. In his usual Sunday service prayers, in the year 1933, he sought god's help for veteran Indian leader and freedom-fighter, Pandit Motilal Nehru, a regular visitor to Mussoorie, who was then seriously ill. There was an immediate hullaballoo in all official tea sessions, and the chaplain was reprimanded. This caused him to comment, 'That in these years of our Lord, Holy Orders can be interpreted to mean wholly Government orders.'

It is easy enough to get to Mussoorie today, but how did visitors manage it before the advent of the railway and the motorcar? It was surely a difficult exercise. Mr Shore and Captain Young merely scrambled up the goat tracks to get here; and Lady Eden used her pony to canter along paths and 'up precipices'; but before that, one detrained at Ghaziabad (near Delhi), engaged a bullock-cart or tonga, and then proceeded in the direction of the Himalayas as speedily as only a bullock-cart or tonga could go. After that, one either walked, rode a pony, or was carried uphill in a doolie, a crude sort of palanquin.

By the turn of the century, the 'Sind, Punjab and Delhi Railway' had got as far as Saharanpur, and the bullock-cart had given way to the dak-ghari.

The only way to reach Dehradun, en route to Mussoorie, was by the dak-ghari or 'night-mail'.

Dak-ghari ponies were different animals, 'always attempting to turn around and get into carriage with the passengers,' as one disgruntled traveller described them. It was only when the coachman used his whip liberally and reviled the ponies' ancestors as far back as three or four generations that the beasts could be persuaded to move. And once they started, there was no stopping them; it was a gallop all the way to the first stage, where the ponies were changed to the accompaniment of a bugle blown by the coachman in true Dickensian fashion.

The journey through the Siwaliks really began—as it still does—at the Mohand Pass. The ascent starts with a gradual gradient, which increases as the road becomes more steep and winding. The hills are abrupt and perpendicular on the southern side, but slope gently away to the north.

At this stage of the journey, drums were beaten (if it was daytime) and torches were lit (if it was night), because frequently wild elephants resented the approach of the dak-ghari and, trumpeting a challenge, would throw the ponies into panic and confusion and send them racing back to the plains.

The railway reached Dehradun in 1901. Till then the main overnight stop was at Rajpur, and the well-known hostelries and forwarding agencies at Rajpur were the 'Ellenborough Hotel', the 'Prince of Wales Hotel', and the 'Agency Retiring Rooms' of Messrs Buckle and Company's 'Bullock Train Agency'. They have long since disappeared. As Dehradun grew in importance, Rajpur's importance dwindled, and for many years its long winding bazaar resembled a ghost-town.

Soon the Savoy and Charleville Hotels opened. Massive furniture, grand-pianos, billiard-tables, barrels of cider and crates of champagne had all come up the hill in lumbering bullock-carts. In 1909, the hotels were suddenly ablaze with light, for this was the year when electricity came to Mussoorie. Before that, the ballrooms and dining-rooms had been hung with chandeliers, the rooms lit by candlelight, and the kitchens with spirit-lamps.

It was after World War I in the 'gay twenties' that the Charleville and the Savoy entered the most popular era, when they were to be as well-known as Raffles in Singapore or the Imperial in Tokyo. Wealthy Indian princes and their families and staff occupied entire wings of the Savoy Hotel. The Savoy Orchestra played every night, and the ballroom was full of couples doing the tango or fox-trot, the latest dancing craze of those days.

After India's Independence in 1947, Mussoorie went through a difficult period. The British had gone, and the wealthy princes and landowners were also finding times difficult. Hotels and boarding-houses began to close down. Then, in the early sixties, the prosperous Indian middle-classes became hill-station conscious, and once again crowds thronged the Mall on summer evenings. These days the foreign tourist is discovering the delights of the lower Himalayas.

Those who wish to move further into the mountains, either on foot or by road, have a wealth of flora and fauna to discover and enjoy. One of the remarkable features of the Himalayas is the abruptness with which they rise from the plains, and this gives them a verdure that is totally different from that of the plains.

None of the common trees of the plains are to be found in the hills. At elevations of 4,000 ft, the long-leaved pine appears. From 5,000 ft there are several kinds of evergreen oak, and above 6,000 ft you find rhododendron, deodar, maple, the hill crypress, and the beautiful horse-chestnut. Still higher up, the silver fir is common; but at 12,000 ft the firs become stunted and dwarfed, and the birch and juniper replace them. At this height raspberries grow wild, amongst yellow colt's-foot dandelion, blue gentian, purple columbine, anemone and edelweiss.

Not every hillside is covered with foliage. Many hills are bare and rugged, too precipitous for cultivation. Sometimes they are masses of quartz, limestone or granite.

Just as the trees of the plains differ from those of the hills, so do the animals and birds. The bear, the goral (a goat-like animal), the marten, the civet-cat, the snow leopard, and the musk-deer, all belong to the Himalayas. The caw of the house-crow is replaced by the deeper note of the corby, and the melodious green hill-pigeon takes the place of the small brown dove.

You do not always see the birds, but you can hear them. As you trek in the interior, or wander along a quiet road in the hill-station, the sound of birds is very pleasant to hear; just as the sound of water in the valleys, the singing of the hill people, the smell of the pines, and the blue smoke rising from the villages, are always with you in the Himalayas.

ALONG THE MANDAKINI

To see a river for the first time at its confluence with another great river is, for me, a special moment in time. And so it was at Rudraprayag, where the waters of the Mandakini joined with the waters of the Alaknanda, the one having come from the glacial snows above Kedarnath, the other from the Himalayan heights beyond Badrinath. Both sacred rivers, both destined to become the holy Ganga further downstream.

I fell in love with the Mandakini at first sight. Or was it the valley that I fell in love with? I am not sure, and it doesn't really matter. The valley is the river.

While the Alaknanda valley, especially in its higher reaches, is a deep and narrow gorge where precipitous outcrops of rock hang threateningly over the traveller, the Mandakini valley is broader, gentler, the terraced fields wider, the banks of the river a green sward in many places. Somehow, one does not feel that one is at the mercy of the Mandakini, whereas one is always at the mercy of the Alaknanda with its sudden landslips and floods.

Rudraprayag is hot. It is probably a pleasant spot in winter, but at the end of June it is decidedly hot. Perhaps its chief claim to fame is that it gave its name to the dreaded man-eating leopard of Rudraprayag who, in the course of seven years (1918–25), accounted for more than three hundred victims. It was finally shot by the fifty-one-year-old Jim Corbett, who recounted the saga of his long hunt for the killer in his fine book, *The Man-Eating Leopard of Rudraprayag.*

The place at which the leopard was shot was the village of Gulabrai, two miles south of Rudraprayag. Under a large mango tree stands a memorial raised to Jim Corbett by officers and men of the Border Roads Organisation. It is a happy gesture to one who loved Garhwal and India. Unfortunately several buffaloes are tethered close by, and one has to wade through slush and buffalo dung to get to the memorial-stone. A board tacked on to the mango tree attracts the attention of motorists, who might pass without noticing the memorial which is off to one side.

The killer leopard was noted for its direct method of attack on humans; and in spite of being poisoned, trapped in a cave, and shot at innumerable times, it did not lose its contempt for man. Two English sportsmen, covering both ends of the old suspension bridge over the Alaknanda, fired several times at the man-eater but to little effect.

It was not long before the leopard acquired a reputation among the hill folk for being an evil spirit. A sadhu was suspected of turning into the leopard by night, and was only saved from being lynched by the ingenuity of Philip Mason, then deputy commissioner of Garhwal. Mason kept the Sadhu in custody until the leopard made his next attack, thus proving the man innocent. Years later, when Mason turned novelist and (using the pen name Philip Woodruffe) wrote *The Wild Sweet Witch*, he had as a character a beautiful young woman who turns into a man-eating leopard by night.

Corbett's host at Gulabrai was one of the few who survived an encounter with the leopard. It left him with a hole in his throat. Apart from being a superb story-teller, Corbett displayed great compassion for people from all walks of life and is still a legend in Garhwal and Kumaon amongst people who have never read his books.

In June one does not linger long in the steamy heat of Rudraprayag. But as one travels up the river, making a gradual ascent of the Mandakini valley, there is a cool breeze coming down from the snows, and the smell of rain is in the air.

The thriving little township of Agastmuni spreads itself along the wide river banks, and further upstream, near a little place called Chandrapuri, we cannot resist breaking our journey to sprawl on the tender green grass that slopes gently down to the swift flowing river. A small rest house is in the making. Around it, banana fronds sway and poplar leaves dance in the breeze.

This is no sluggish river of the plains, but a fast-moving current tumbling over rocks, turning and twisting in its efforts to discover the easiest way for its frothy snow-fed waters to escape the mountains. Escape is the word, for the constant plaint of many a Garhwali is that, while his hills abound in rivers, the water runs down and away and little, if any, reaches the fields and villages above it. Cultivation must depend on the rain and not on the river.

The road climbs gradually, still keeping to the river. Just outside Guptakashi, my attention is drawn to a clump of huge trees sheltering a small but ancient temple. We stop here and enter the shade of the trees.

The temple is deserted. It is a temple dedicated to Shiva, and in the courtyard are several river-rounded stone lingams on which leaves and blossoms have fallen. No one seems to come here, which is strange, since it is on the pilgrim route. Two boys from a neighbouring field leave their yoked bullocks to come and talk to me, but they cannot tell me much about the temple except to confirm that it is seldom visited. 'The buses do not stop here.' That seems explanation enough. For where the buses go, the pilgrims go; and where the pilgrims go, other pilgrims will follow. Thus far and no further.

The trees seem to be magnolias. But I have never seen magnolia trees grow to such huge proportions. Perhaps they are something else. Never mind; let them remain a sweet-scented mystery.

Guptakashi in the evening is all abustle. A coachload of pilgrims (headed for Kedarnath) has just arrived, and the tea-shops near the bus-stand are doing brisk business. Then the 'local' bus from Ukhimath, across the river, arrives and many of the passengers head for a tea-shop famed for its samosas. The local bus is called the Bhook-Hartal, the 'Hunger-strike' bus.

'How did it get that name?' I asked one of the samosa-eaters.

'Well, it's an interesting story. For a long time we had been asking the authorities to provide a bus service for the local people and for the villagers who live off the roads. All the buses came from Srinagar or Rishikesh and were taken up by pilgrims. The locals could't find room on them. But our pleas went unheard until the whole town, or most of it, anyway decided to go on hunger-strike. That worked! And so the bus is named after our successful hunger-strike.'

'They nearly put me out of business too,' said the tea-shop owner cheerfully 'Nobody ate any samosas for two days!'

There is no cinema or public place of entertainment at Guptakashi, and the town goes to sleep early and wakes early.

At six, the hillside, green from recent rain, sparkles in the morning sunshine. The snow-capped Chaukhamba (7,140 metres) is dazzling. The air is clear; no smoke or dust up here. The climate, I am told, is mild all the year round, judging by the scent and shape of the flowers, and the boys call them Champa (Hindi for magnolia blossom). Ukhimath, on the other side of the river, lies in the shadow. It gets the sun at nine. In winter it must wait till afternoon. And yet it seems a bigger place, and by tradition the temple priests from Kedarnath winter there when the snows cover that distant shrine.

Guptakashi has not yet been rendered ugly by the barrack type architecture that has come up in some growing hill towns. The old double-storeyed houses are built of stone, with grey slate roofs. They blend well with the hillside. Cobbled paths meander through the old bazaar.

One of these takes up to the famed Guptakashi temple, tucked away above the old part of the town. Here, as in Benares, Shiva is worshipped as Vishwanath, and two underground streams representing the sacred Jumna and Bhagirathi rivers feed the pool sacred to the god. This temple gives the town its name—Gupta-Kashi, the 'Invisible Benares', just as Uttarkashi on the Bhagirathi is 'Upper Benares'.

Guptakashi and its environs has so many lingams that the saying *'Jitne kankar utne Shankar'*—'as many stones, so many Shivas'—has become a proverb to describe its holiness.

From Guptakashi, pilgrims proceed north to Kedarnath, and the last stage of their journey—about a day's march—must be covered on foot or horseback. The temple of Kedarnath, situated at a height of 11,753 ft, is encircled by snow-capped peaks, and Atkinson has conjectured that 'the symbol of the linga may have arisen from the pointed peaks around his (God Shiva's) original home'.

The temple is dedicated to Sadashiva, the subterranean form of the god, who, 'fleeing from the Pandavas took refuge here in the form of a he-buffalo and finding himself hard-pressed, dived into the ground leaving the hinder parts on the surface, which continue to be the subject of adoration.'

The other portions of the god are worshipped as follows: the arms at Tungnath, at a height of 13,000 ft; the face at Rudranath

(12,000 ft); the belly at Madmaheshwar, eighteen miles north-east of Guptakashi; and the hair and head at Kalpeshwar, near Joshimath. These five sacred shrines form the Panch Kedars (five Kedars).

We leave the Mandakini to visit Tungnath on the Chandrashila range. But I will return to this river. It has captured my mind and heart.

www.ingramcontent.com/pod-product-compliance
Lightning Source LLC
LaVergne TN
LVHW090526110826
845146LV00003B/991

* 9 7 8 9 3 6 1 5 6 4 2 8 4 *